D0020039

Stacey's Book

**Other books by
Ann M. Martin**

Rachel Parker, Kindergarten Show-off

Eleven Kids, One Summer

Ma and Pa Dracula

Yours Turly, Shirley

Ten Kids, No Pets

Slam Book

Just a Summer Romance

Missing Since Monday

With You and Without You

Me and Katie (the Pest)

Stage Fright

Inside Out

Bummer Summer

BABY-SITTERS LITTLE SISTER series
THE BABY-SITTERS CLUB mysteries
THE BABY-SITTERS CLUB series

THE BABY-SITTERS CLUB

Stacey's Book

Ann M. Martin

AN
APPLE
PAPERBACK

SCHOLASTIC INC.
New York Toronto London Auckland Sydney

*The author gratefully acknowledges
Jeanne Betancourt
for her help in
preparing this manuscript.*

*Macy's is a Federally Registered Trademark of
R. H. Macy and Co., Inc.*

Hard Rock Cafe button used with permission.

*If you purchased this book without a cover, you should be aware that this book
is stolen property. It was reported as "unsold and destroyed" to the publisher,
and neither the author nor the publisher has received any payment for this
"stripped book."*

No part of this publication may be reproduced in whole or in part,
or stored in a retrieval system, or transmitted in any form or by any
means, electronic, mechanical, photocopying, recording, or other-
wise, without written permission of the publisher. For information
regarding permission, write to Scholastic Inc., 555 Broadway, New
York, NY 10012.

ISBN 0-590-48399-4

Copyright © 1994 by Ann M. Martin. All rights reserved. Published
by Scholastic Inc. THE BABY-SITTERS CLUB ® and APPLE
PAPERBACKS ® are registered trademarks of Scholastic Inc.

12 11 10 9 8 7 6 5 4 3 2   5 6 7 8 9/9

Printed in the U.S.A.

First Scholastic printing, November 1994

CHAPTER 1

"Hello, room." I know it sounds cutesy to say hello to a room. It *is* cutesy. But I'm so happy to be home, it just came out. Do you know that feeling? It's the end of a busy day. You get home and the first thing you do is make a quick stop in the kitchen to grab something to eat. But then you go right to your room and close the door behind you. You look around and feel so great just being there.

I'm Stacey McGill, by the way. I have long wavy blonde hair (it's a perm), blue eyes, and I'm tall for my age (thirteen). Today, at this moment, I'm wearing black tights, a pink-and-black striped oversized sweat shirt, and pink high-top sneakers. Oh, yes, and right now I'm smiling because I heard myself saying hi to my room. My room is "wearing" lace curtains, a brass bed with a blue satin quilt, a second-hand bureau that my mom and I painted white, my desk, and a flower patterned rug.

I know that some people don't have their own rooms and maybe not even a place to live, which makes me even more grateful that I have my own room. Make that *rooms*. You see, I have two bedrooms but not in the same house. It's all because my parents are divorced. My other bedroom is in New York City where I go to be with my dad on some weekends and during some vacations. The rest of the time — which is most of the time — I live with my mother in Stoneybrook, Connecticut, where I have this room.

My parents are as different from each other as you can imagine two people to be, so it makes sense (even to me) that they'd be divorced. I used to worry that the parts of me that are like each of them would clash inside of me and give me personality problems. I'd have this fight going on inside me between the part that's like my father (being a workaholic) and the part that's like my mother (being laid back). But it doesn't work out that way. The characteristics I have from each of them seem to balance in me. I work hard, like my father, especially at my school work (I love math) and on my baby-sitting jobs (which I love too). But I also love to have a good time. So I spend plenty of time hanging out with my friends and enjoying life in Stoneybrook — like my mom. And, also like my mom, I love to shop.

Which brings up another major thing about me. I like to dress nicely and look good. My Stoneybrook friends all say I have style. Frankly I think that if I have "style" it's because I grew up in New York City. In case you don't know it, New York City is the style-capital of America, if not the world. I don't mean to sound snobby, because honest I'm not. It's just a fact. But I ♥ New York City for more than the great fashions and the stores that sell them. I also like to do "city things," such as go to museums and plays or just walk on the crowded streets. New York City is so interesting and exciting that going for a walk can be a major event.

Even though I go to New York City a lot to see my dad, if you asked me where I live I'd most definitely say in Stoneybrook. I moved to Stoneybrook with both my parents at the beginning of seventh grade, when my dad got an opportunity to work there for his company. My parents thought because of my diabetes it would be good for me to live in a sleepy little town. (By the way, being a diabetic means that my blood sugar has to be checked every day and I have to give myself insulin shots. I also have to count calories and I can't eat sugar.)

3

Well, Stoneybrook turned out not to be a sleepy little town at all. My new friends and I make sure of that. We have a club (the Baby-sitters Club or BSC) and go to a great school (Stoneybrook Middle School or SMS). I'm not saying that Stoneybrook is exciting like New York City, but it's a fabulous place to live and I luv it.

Speaking of luv, I've already had a few boy-friends. I can't say that any of them has been the passion of my life. But my most recent boyfriend, Robert Brewster, just might be. He's incredibly sensitive and sweet.

For me, having a boyfriend doesn't take away from my other friendships. Because while I'm falling in and out of luv with different guys my friends in the Baby-sitters Club are my constant friends. We all know each other so well and trust each other so much that we can tell one another anything. We also give each other great advice.

Let me tell you just a little bit about my friends.

First and foremost, there's Claudia Kishi — my best friend. Claud is tall, has the best skin, and long, silky dark hair. She's Japanese-American and is what my mother would call "a great beauty." When Claud comes to New York City she fits right in because she wears very funky clothes and has style with a capital "S."

The other thing about Claudia is that she's an absolutely amazing artist. She can make something beautiful out of any old thing. Hand her a paper clip and she'll hand you back a wire sculpture of a cat. And she makes awesome earrings out of scraps of this and that. The rest of us Baby-sitters Club members give her our old and broken jewelry and she remakes it into great new jewelry. Claudia Kishi has talent with a capital "T." Though she'd probably spell it "t-a-l-l-a-n-t." (She hates schoolwork and is a terrible speller.)

Kristy Thomas is the one who thought of the Baby-sitters Club in the first place. As our president she is efficient and bossy enough to keep the BSC business running smoothly. Another thing about Kristy is that she loves sports so much that she organized and runs a softball team for kids called the Krushers. Kristy is the most take-charge person I know.

Then there are Mary Anne Spier and Dawn Schafer. I put them together because they live in the same house. You see Mary Anne's father married Dawn's mother. Mary Anne and Dawn are really glad because they were best friends before their parents got married, and now they're sisters, too. Dawn's mother and father are divorced, so Dawn and I are both dealing with the big "D" — Divorce. The other thing Dawn and I have in common is that neither of us eats junk food. Dawn doesn't because she's into eating only food that's good for you. I don't eat junk food because of my diabetes. A chocolate bar still looks excellent and tempting to me, but I know (from experience) that if I don't resist I could get very, very sick. Right now Dawn is on a leave of absence from the Baby-sitters Club. She decided to go to California and live with her father and brother for awhile. I really miss her.

Shannon Kilbourne, who used to be an associate member of BSC, is taking Dawn's place.

The other two regular members of the Baby-sitters Club are sixth-graders. Some girls in my school are snobby about hanging out with anyone who's in a lower grade than they are, but not my friends. So two of our members (and best friends) are Jessi Ramsey and Mallory Pike.

Mal loves to write. She has an amazing number of brothers (four) and sisters (three). If I'm ever a little sad about being an only child I go over to the Pikes' and get a good dose of life with a big family. Then, when I get home, I really appreciate the peace and quiet of life alone with my mom.

Jessi is this awesome ballet dancer. She gets up before five-thirty every morning to practice, in addition to going to Stamford two times a week for lessons. She's had roles in *Nutcracker*, *Swan Lake*, and *Coppélia*. If you've seen Jessi dance you'd believe her when she says she's going to be a professional dancer some day.

Claudia, Kristy, Dawn, Mary Anne, and Mallory were the new friends I made when we moved to Stoneybrook. (I didn't meet Jessi until later.) Then guess what happened? My dad got transferred *back* to New York City and I had to say good-bye to my new friends.

In New York City we had to get a new apartment because our old apartment had been rented to someone else. At least I got to go back to my old private school with my old friends (including Laine who is now my ex-best friend, but that's another story). We had been in New York for only a short while when my parents decided that the solution to their problems with one another was to get a divorce. They said it was up to me to decide which parent I wanted to live with.

That's right. It was my decision, the hardest one I've ever made. I chose to live with my mom and we moved back to Stoneybrook. The house we'd lived in had been bought by Jessi Ramsey's family. We didn't mind because the house was too big and expensive for just the two of us. We ended up buying a small, run-down house which we fixed up. Now we think it's just perfect.

As I'm telling you this I realize that both times we moved to Stoneybrook it was because of one of the big "Ds" in my life. The first time was because of my Diabetes and the second time because of the Divorce. But the second time I moved here without the good "D" in my life — Dad. I miss him.

But even with all the problems I've had with the two "Ds," I'd say I'm a happy person. Also, between living in two places, being a member of the Baby-sitters Club, having all these great friends to hang out with, and dealing with being diabetic, I'm a busy person.

I'm going on like this, telling you about me, not because I'm conceited (I don't think I am; I sure hope not), but because I have this school assignment to think and write about myself. See if you can guess what it is. That's right. I have to write my autobiography.

Everyone in the eighth grade of SMS has to write one. It's been interesting to think through my life this far. I've been trying to remember the past while I look through old photo albums and school stuff my mother saved.

For the section I call "My Early Years" I had to ask my parents lots of questions. They got all teary-eyed and smiley when I asked them about when I was a baby. Probably because I'm an only child and I have this serious disease.

So here I am on my bed, eating cottage cheese (no sugar, remember?), loving my room, and ready to go to work on my autobiography. I'm about to proofread what I've written so far. . . .

THE AUTOBIOGRAPHY OF ANASTASIA (STACEY) McGILL THE EARLY YEARS

CHAPTER 2

I was born at 1:30 AM on April 3 in Mt. Sinai Hospital, New York City. I don't remember anything about coming into the world. But my father and mother remember it well and say I was a happy baby and that I smiled at them right away. I know that's hard to believe since everyone says babies don't smile for the first couple of weeks. But they swear I flashed them this big smile as soon as I came into the world.

My dad says he doesn't understand how anyone could say newborns are ugly, because I was the most beautiful thing he ever saw. I've seen my baby pictures so I can't say I agree with him. I guess it's like a kid loving a Cabbage Patch doll.

One of the reasons I don't think I was very cute is because I had practically no hair. You couldn't see the little that I did have because it was blonde. My mother says she wasn't worried at all about my hair growing, but I read in the baby book she kept about me that she used to rub my head because she thought it would help my hair grow. She wrote down everything about me at first. Things like who came to visit me and what presents they brought. She even wrote down my eating schedule. There are pages and pages of details that I will spare the reader of this autobiography.

Let's move ahead several months to the entry on the page titled: "Baby's First Step" where my mother wrote:

At ten months Anastasia took her first steps. She was

standing at the coffee table when her daddy came home from work. He said, "Come to Daddy." She let go of the coffee table and took two steps before she realized that she wasn't holding on to anything. She looked from one of us to the other as if to say, "Am I really doing this? Am I okay?" She started to teeter. But with encouragement from her daddy she regained her balance and took a few more steps to reach his arms. She's still wobbly on her feet.

I guess I got over that wobbly business pretty quickly because the next entry in the book is:

Eleven months. Stacey is running everywhere and getting into everything. She's a very active child. I can't leave her for a minute

Goobaw and me at one year.
Friends forever.

That was the last entry my mother made in my baby book. When I asked her why she didn't fill in the other pages, she said she was too busy trying to keep up with me.

But she does remember that I started talking long before I was two years old. She managed to make a list of my first words and still keep an eye on me. Instead of putting them in my baby book every time I said a new word, she added it to a list she'd stuck to the refrigerator door with alphabet magnets. She wrote down about twenty-five words before she finally quit doing it.

I saw on the list that like most kids my first word was "Ma-ma" and my second was "Da-Da."

The third word I said was "Bih-bih," which my mother tells me was my way of saying "Big Bird." I loved *Sesame Street*.

The fourth word I spoke was "Cha," which means chair. If I wanted to say "rocking chair" I waved my hand as I said "Cha." I don't remember any of this so I have to take her word for it.

The next word is "Goobaw," which is what I still call my teddy bear. Nobody knows why I named him that, least of all me. By the way, you wouldn't for a second recognize Goobaw as the same teddy as in my baby pictures. Now Goobaw only has one eye and his fur is practically worn off. I rubbed my teddy the way my mother rubbed my head. But in the case of Goobaw it had the opposite effect.

I still hold onto Goobaw when I'm sad. And every time I've been in the hospital for my diabetes you can bet Goobaw went with me.

When I was three years old we moved from Greenwich Village to an apartment on the Upper East Side. The move is the first memory I have. I guess it must have been traumatic for me. Now that I've moved three times in two years I can tell you moving is still traumatic for me.

So here's my first memory.

I was in my bedroom playing with wooden blocks when my mother came into my room carrying big, empty cardboard boxes. I looked up at her and she said something like, "Stacey, we've got to pack your things. Let's do it together."

At first it was fun to put my toys in the boxes. It was like playing with them. But when she taped the boxes closed and told me again, "We're moving," I didn't feel happy at all. I was confused. She let me keep out Goobaw and a few other toys, but I thought that the rest of my toys were gone forever. I was terribly frightened and I didn't know how to explain that to my mother.

That's all I remember about the move. The rest of my childhood memories take place in the uptown apartment, which (by the way) I loved.

Another early memory is of going to pre-school in my new neighborhood. One beautiful spring day my dad took me to school. When we got outside he bent over and put me up on his shoulders. Instead of being on an eye level with garbage cans and people's knees, I was taller than everyone we passed. I loved it. My dad was in a hurry to get to work on time so he walked fast, which was even more fun for me. I put my chin on his head and (I actually remember feeling this) thought about how much fun I was having.

Here's a memory I have of being in pre-school. It couldn't have been the same day as the on-Dad's-shoulders memory, because I remember it was raining. One of my classmates, Petey, had a messy cubby next to my neat one. And if his stuff wouldn't fit in his cubby, he'd stick the overflow in mine.

This rainy day that I remember so well Petey put his muddy boots in my cubby on top of a book I'd brought for Show and Share Time. The book was *Eloise*, and it was my prized possession. Two wet, muddy footprints were on the cover of my beloved Eloise. I was so mad at Petey that I wanted to kick him and hit him and bite him. Then, after I punished him myself, I was going to tell the teacher. But since I didn't want anyone to see that I was crying I couldn't do any of those things to Petey. So I hid in my cubby.

It was a tight squeeze, but once I got myself all folded up it was cozy. I decided that from then on, when I came to that dumb old school with dumb old kids like Petey, I would go right to my cubby and stay there until it was time to go home. From the cubby I could see that Lydia and Pam were playing with my favorite things from the dress-up trunk — princess dresses. But I didn't care. I wasn't budging.

I don't remember anything else about that incident. But I do remember that except for that day I loved preschool, so it's a safe bet that I didn't spend the rest of the year in the cubby.

By the way, the cover of my copy of *Eloise* is still wrinkled and stained from Petey's boot marks. As it turned out Petey later went to Parker, the school I attended from kindergarten until I moved to Stoneybrook. Petey was one of my good friends at Parker but I'd still never want to share a locker with him. No one would. At the end of sixth grade he won the award for the most dirty sweat socks (stink-socks?) in a locker. Petey had thirty-one of them.

During those early years, on weekends my parents and I would do all sorts of things in the city. (If my dad had to work my mom and I would go off by ourselves.) I especially remember going to Central Park. We'd put a blanket down in Sheep Meadow. There aren't any sheep in the meadow, but there used to be long before any of us was born. Anyway, we'd sit on the blanket in Sheep(less) Meadow and watch all the people. I'd color or look at books or just run around like kids do, while my mother (and father, if he was there) read the Sunday *New York Times*. I liked it best when we went with another family so I'd have a kid or two to play with.

Oh, and here's a neat thing. In Sheep Meadow there was usually someone playing bongo drums or a guitar. And outside the Meadow people with pushcarts were selling cold drinks, ice cream, and pretzels. Those were the good old days when I could have sugar. I always chose an ice cream on a stick with chocolate covering. Yummy!

Another thing I loved to do when I was little was go to the Museum of Natural History. I never tired of doing that (though I bet after awhile my parents did). I love all the big glass cases with exhibits of stuffed animals. Each one is set up in the appropriate environment for the animal. So if you're looking at a rhinoceros there's a little stuffed bird on its back. The thing is, it's exactly the bird that would stand on a rhino's back in nature. The plants are the same as they would be in nature, too. The point is that you know that whatever is behind that glass wall is what you would see if you came across a rhino in the wild. It's all been carefully researched.

Sometimes I'd be looking at one exhibit and over my shoulder I'd think I saw an animal in another case *moving*! I was always a little scared when I walked around that section of the Museum of Natural History. But that was part of what I liked. It made it so exciting.

I did not find nightmares exciting though, and I had a lot of scary ones when I was around four years old. My mother remembers them, too. When I cried out she'd come as fast as she could. To help me get over being scared, she'd ask me what I was dreaming. Then she'd stay with me until I fell asleep again. We talked about those nightmares recently and we both agreed that there were monsters in them. She said I often mentioned something scary coming in my window. And I remember dreaming that there was something horrid under my bed. I thought that if I got out of bed it would grab me. But if I didn't get out of the bed it would rise up and fly out the window with me and my bed on its back. (This may have been about the time I first saw *Peter Pan*.)

Having nightmares when I was a little kid makes me very sympathetic with my baby-sitting charges. I always make sure when they're asleep that the house is quiet enough so I'll hear them if they cry or call out.

The clearest memory of my early years was the day of my fourth birthday when my parents took me to the Plaza Hotel. The Plaza is just about the fanciest and most famous hotel in the world. It is right on Central Park and lots of movies are shot there. It is so, so elegant.

I already told you that when I was in pre-school Eloise was my favorite storybook character. Here's the connection between Eloise and the Plaza Hotel. Eloise lives there with her Nanny, her dog Weenie, and her turtle Skipperdee.

Since the Plaza is home to Eloise, she roams all over the hotel. She runs up and down halls, gets on and off elevators, and hangs out in places other guests in the hotel don't even know about. She also calls room service a lot, making sure to order roast-beef bones for Weenie, and raisins for Skipperdee. Eloise is a lively and mischievous girl. So you can see why at four she was my hero.

When I learned that my mother and father were taking me to the Plaza Hotel to celebrate my birthday I was terrifically excited. I picked out a skirt with straps to hold it up, like the one Eloise wears in the book. I wanted to leave my hair uncombed and stringy and have bangs cut (just like Eloise's) but my mother drew the line there.

My parents also dressed up (and combed their hair) for lunch at the Plaza. My father wore his best suit and tie and my mother topped off her dressy outfit with a hat with a veil.

As we walked through the Plaza lobby my parents said they wanted to show me a painting.

I said, "But I don't want to see a painting. I want to go on the elevator and run up and down the halls like Eloise did."

"You just come with us," my dad said. "I think you will like this painting."

They took me down a hall and showed me a huge painting of Eloise. I just stood there in amazement. I loved it. It made me believe more than ever that Eloise was real.

And lunch in the Palm Court was so fancy. There were the big palms everywhere. (That's why it's called the "Palm Court.") The tables were covered with pink tablecloths and set with gold-trimmed dishes. A lady in an evening gown was playing a harp. The whole experience was so special that I was breathless. The food was good, too.

Just when I was eyeing the dessert table and trying to decide which chocolaty thing I would order, a waiter appeared before me holding out a perfect little chocolate cake with a lit sparkler in the middle. My mother and father and the waiters started singing "Happy Birthday" to me. It seemed as if everyone eating lunch at the Palm Court joined in. And amid all the voices there was this big, booming, wonderful voice.

While the waiter was cutting the cake into threes for us, he told me that a famous opera singer was having lunch there, too. That was the voice we heard. Pavarotti had sung "Happy Birthday" to me! We decided not to bother him by asking for his autograph.

After lunch my parents finally took me upstairs in the elevator so I could see if the halls looked like the ones in *Eloise*. They did, exactly. Red carpets and all. The person who wrote those books did careful research. (Don't expect the halls to look like that now, because the Plaza Hotel has been completely redecorated since then.)

Anyway, when we stepped off the elevator I couldn't resist running. Just like Eloise, I tore down the hall and screeched around a corner to come face-to-face with a room service cart piled high with food. Behind the cart was a startled waiter. I missed knocking into him and his cart by the tiniest bit. Even though I scared him, he remained calm. "My, my," he said. "I see we have an Eloise up here today."

"I'm sorry," I said. I was so embarrassed (and frightened) that I turned around and walked as fast as I could back to the elevator where my parents were waiting for me.

Later I wished I had told the waiter, "I'm very busy today. And I need some raisins for Skipperdee. Could you kindly send some up right away and charge it, please?"

As we left the Plaza, just when I was thinking that my wonderful birthday celebration was over, my father hired a horse-drawn carriage. I can still picture it. The horse was white. The driver had long red hair and wore a black tuxedo and a high hat. The sky was bright blue on this perfect sunshiny spring afternoon. *Clip clop. Clip clop.* We went all around Central Park.

My fourth birthday was my favorite birthday celebration of all.

Central Park, New York City. My first ride in a horsedrawn carriage.

WHEN I WAS FIVE

CHAPTER 3

"And they lived happily ever after."
Lots of fairy tales end that way. When
I was five years old I learned that
not every story in real life has a
happy ending. I think this is one of
the things you begin to learn when
you're about five. If you're lucky you
also learn that sometimes the story
just isn't over yet.

```
To: Parker Academy Students
    Classes begin on Wednesday,
    September 10 at 9:00 A.M.
            Anastasia McGill
_____is in
Miss Moss's Kindergarten
which meets in Room_____.
                          130
```

I felt so grown-up when I got this card!

Starting at five I have lots of memories. For example, I remember the first day of kindergarten. I was really nervous because I was going to a new school. It was a *big* school with *big* kids, even high school kids. I held on tight to my mother's hand as we walked through the front door of Parker.

The first person I saw when I came into the bright classroom (which was also *big*) was Petey Squires — Ole Muddy Feet Pete. You can imagine my disappointment. The only other person I recognized was Laine Cummings.

Laine hadn't been at my preschool, but our parents knew one another so we'd played together a few times. I think I might have been the *only* other kid Laine knew at Parker because she came right over when she saw my mother and me.

My mother said, "Hi, Laine." Then she squatted down to be at our height and said, "Isn't this nice that you two are in the same class? I hope you'll become very good friends."

"Oh, yeah," Laine said. "Sure. Why not?" Even then Laine acted cool and as if nothing fazed her.

A little later our teacher, Miss Moss, told us to sit in a circle around her to begin the school day. I was at my new cubby checking out if it was big enough to fit into in case of an emergency. But I could see Laine running right over to the teacher and sitting down on the circle rug before any of the other kids.

As I made my way past the tables and chairs toward the circle I heard Laine tell another girl who wanted to sit next to her, "This place is saved for Stacey." It made me feel very special. By the way, the girl was Deirdre, who became another good friend of mine.

In a week or so I realized that I wouldn't need to hide in my cubby. I loved kindergarten. We'd settled into our school routines and I was getting to know (and like) the new kids, mostly other girls. And Miss Moss was terrific. She spent time every day teaching us songs and games that were more grown-up than the ones I learned in preschool. A lot of the games and songs I teach the kids I baby-sit for now I learned in kindergarten. (Thank you, Miss Moss.)

One afternoon, after we played an alphabet game, Miss Moss told us to sit in the Story Circle. She sat on the rug with us, held up a hardcover book and asked, "Who knows the story of *Cinderella*?"

About half the kids raised their hands and called out, "I do. I do." Laine raised her hand, too. She looked at me sitting there with my hands on my lap and said, "Stacey. Put your hand up." The name Cinderella was familiar, but I didn't know her story so I put my hand half in the air.

I stared at the cover of the book with the beautiful red-haired girl in a blue gown while Miss Moss quieted everyone down. "Well,"

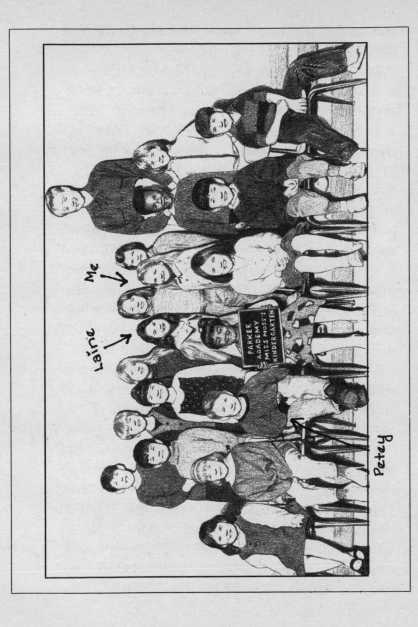

A great teacher, and a bunch of nice kids.

she said, "if you all know the story, do you think I should still read it?"

My heart stopped beating. Maybe Miss Moss wouldn't read the book and I'd never know about Cinderella and what happens to her.

Everyone yelled out, "Read it." And, "I want to hear it again." I joined by shouting, "Please read it. Please, Miss Moss."

The next thing I knew the story was over and I had been in another land with a beautiful girl who is cruelly treated by extremely mean stepsisters. Cinderella's luck changes from bad to good with the help of a powerful fairy god-mother and animal friends who talk. She's also lucky enough to fall in love with a prince who's good at finding people. Of course, she and the prince live happily ever after. I loved it.

When Laine and I were getting our coats and stuff from our side-by-side cubbies she said, "How come you didn't know about Cinderella?"

"I knew a little bit," I said.

Laine smiled, "Of course you did. Every kid knows about Cinderella. The movie is opening next week. It's been rereleased." (Even at five Laine talked like that. Her dad is this big deal producer of Broadway plays so she grew up around show business talk.) Then she said, "There's a preview on Saturday. My dad's got two free tickets. I'll tell him you should come with me."

"What's a preview?" I asked.

"It's when they invite the critics and important people," she explained. "Like my dad."

The next day, true to her word, Laine told me that her mom would call my mom and we'd go to the movie together.

Previews are great fun. Over the years I've been to a lot of movie and theater previews with Laine. You just show your pass at the door and sail right in. Everyone's in a cheerful mood because they get to go to the movie for free and see it before anyone else. Seeing that preview was the most grown-up thing that I'd done in my life so far. And the movie was wonderful.

When I got home my mother had a surprise for me. She'd been to the library to return some books and had borrowed a copy of *Cinderella* and an audiotape of the soundtrack from the movie. I played that tape over and over and over. Finally my mother said, "Really, Stacey, you're going to wear it out." Now that I think about it, my mom must have been sick of listening to all the songs over and over. I know that's how I feel when the kids I baby-sit for can't get enough of one of their tapes or discs.

Anyway, Monday morning when Laine and I were putting our jackets in our cubbies, she asked me, "Did you like the movie?"

"It's real good," I said. I didn't tell her I knew the whole soundtrack by heart.

After school each day that week as soon as I got home I'd sing along with the soundtrack to *Cinderella* and look at the pictures in the book.

Now, about then my mother started a part-time job in the children's clothing department at Macy's. Her job probably marked the beginning of my being so interested in clothes. She had an employees' discount so she was always bringing me home new outfits. I'd try them on and unless she and I decided that a sweater or a skirt or a whatever looked perfect on me, she'd take it back to the store the next day and bring me home something different. It was the best kind of home shopping.

But there was something even better about her job at Macy's that I didn't know about until a week before Thanksgiving.

"How would you like to be in the Thanksgiving Day parade?" she asked me one night at dinner.

"What a great idea," my father said. "We'll make a Stacey balloon. The Stacey McGill balloon floating down Central Park West."

"The parade with Kermit the Frog?" I asked my mother.

My mother was laughing at my father's idea

of a Stacey balloon so she didn't quite hear me. "What frog?" she asked.

"Kermit. In the parade," I answered.

"Yes," my mother said. "The Thanksgiving Day parade. It's the *Macy's* Thanksgiving Day parade. So people who work at Macy's are in it. The people who hold onto the balloon strings and the people on the floats all work at Macy's. The children in the parade are the children of people who work at Macy's. Would you like to be in the parade?"

"Instead of watching it?" I asked. I was having trouble following what she was talking about. Especially because my father was still joking about my being a balloon.

"Stacey for Macy's," he said, "It has a ring, don't you think?"

"Anyway," my mother said. "I signed you up, Stacey. To be on the *Cinderella* float. I thought you'd like that, and they were looking for girls to ride on the float."

"I'll be with Cinderella?" I asked. "The real one?"

"As real as she gets," my father said.

My mother was smiling. "I guess I made the right choice, huh? I sort of figured out that you love Cinderella."

"I do," was all I could say.

The next day I told Laine I was going to

meet Cinderella and be in the Thanksgiving Day parade. She was pretty impressed. She also knew a lot more than I did about being in a parade.

"It's going to be cold out there," she warned me. "But they probably won't let you wear a coat or anything. You have to smile anyway. Everyone does. And wave your hand like this." She demonstrated a smile and a wave. "It's important to smile because you're going to be on television," she said. "Millions of people will see you."

I'd been so excited about meeting Cinderella that I hadn't thought about the parade being televised.

I wanted to ask Laine why I couldn't wear a coat and still smile and wave, but she'd run over to Miss Moss to tell her my big news.

After lunch that day Miss Moss had us sit in the circle for Talk Time. "So Stacey has some big news to share with us today," she said.

Everyone looked at me.

"I'm going to be in the Macy's Thanksgiving Day parade," I said, "with Cinderella."

The kids were so excited they started talking at once. But they listened when Laine said, "And she'll be on TV."

"We'll all watch for you," Miss Moss said. "Won't we, boys and girls?"

All the kids in my class said they would.

We talked about the parade some more. Miss Moss told us what was in the parade balloons to make them float. After that she asked each of us to say which balloon we liked best and what characters we'd like to see as balloons. I said, "Cinderella." Laine said, "Madonna."

That day after school I put on the televison and thought about how I was going to be on TV. My mother came into the living room and asked, "What are you watching, Stacey?"

I was so busy thinking that I didn't know what it was I was watching. I guess it wasn't a good show for a kid to be watching because my mother turned it off. "Really, Stacey," she said, "can't you find something more interesting to do?"

I asked her, "How many more days until Thanksgiving?"

That night before I went to sleep I looked at the drawing of Cinderella on the cover of the book and told her I'd see her in six days.

On the day before Thanksgiving we had a party at school for our parents. My dad had to be at work, but my mom and Laine's mother and lots of other mothers and fathers came to school to have a special potluck lunch with us. My mother made candied sweet potatoes. I don't remember what Laine and her mother brought, but I do remember that Miss Moss made a big turkey. Our parents looked at the art we'd displayed around the room. There was a whole section of collages based on our favorite storybook characters. Guess what character I chose? Yup, Cinderella.

After lunch we made a circle big enough to include our parents and sang a couple of Thanksgiving Day songs, then a lot of other songs. Miss Moss seemed to know just which ones our parents would be able to join in on, such as "Michael Rowed the Boat Ashore."

Before we broke up to go home for our four-day vacation Miss Moss said, "Now don't forget, class. Stacey will be in the Thanksgiving Day parade. If you watch it on TV keep an eye out for her."

"I'll be standing right next to Cinderella," I added. "I'll wave to you."

That day we took longer than usual saying good-bye. Four days seemed like such a long time to be apart and we'd all had so much fun at the party. Laine and two of my other friends and their mothers were standing in front of the school talking. Deirdre said to me, "You're going to be in the parade. My cousins and me are going to watch you on TV."

It was getting crowded on the sidewalk with all the older kids coming out of the building so we wished one another "Happy Thanksgiving," and said our good-byes.

Deidre, who was already walking away with her mother, turned around and yelled to me, "Have fun in the parade. Don't forget to wave to me."

A couple of big girls who were passing heard her and stopped in front of me. "Hey," one of them said. I looked up at her as she asked me, "Are you going to be in the parade?"

"Yes," I answered. "With Cinderella. On her float."

"Awesome," the other one said.

"A celebrity in our own school," the first one said. She was probably being a little sarcastic, but I was too young to pick it up.

Laine's mother and my mother had finally finished saying good-bye to one another. Just as they were ready to walk away, Laine said to me, "I hope it doesn't rain for the parade."

I asked my mother, "What if it rains?"

"You can always carry an umbrella," my mother said. "But don't worry about it. The forecast for tomorrow is unseasonably warm and sunny."

"Great," I said.

CHAPTER 4

When I got up the morning of the parade it was still too early to know if it would be a sunny day or not. If you're in the parade you have to be there really early. That gives the people who organize the parade time to be sure everyone is there and in the right place to start marching at nine A.M. sharp. With all those floats, balloons, bands, and clowns, organization is a big thing.

My mother was staying home to make Thanksgiving dinner for us and my aunt Beverly, uncle Lou, and my cousins Jonathan and Kirsten. She got up with us to make me a big breakfast and put the turkey in the oven.

"I'm glad I'm staying home," she said as she put a plate of scrambled eggs and toast in front of me. "I want to be watching with the rest of the world when my little girl is on television."

"And you're going to tape it, right?" I asked.

"Right."

I was too excited to be very hungry, but my father said I had a long and busy morning ahead of me so I'd better "chow down."

"Will I be on television the whole time?" I asked.

"Just when the float gets to Herald Square in front of Macy's," my mother explained. "You'll know when you get there. First you'll see the big store. And across the street from Macy's you'll see lots of lights and cameras. If you stay close to Cinderella you're bound to be on television because the TV cameras will want to get some good shots of her."

"I'm going to smile and wave the whole time, though," I told them. "For all the people along the parade route."

I was learning a lot about the Thanksgiving Day parade. But I had a whole lot more to learn. For instance, if your mother tells you to wear your coat, do it. Even on an unseasonably warm day it can be windy and chilly when you're outdoors for hours just standing around waiting for the parade to begin. I was glad I had my coat on.

The float was beautiful. It was designed to look like the fancy coach that takes Cinderella to the ball, and was drawn by four white horses. Cinderella wasn't there yet. Just me, five other girls who were older than me, and

waiting ... and waiting for Cinderella.

a woman from Macy's who was responsible for taking care of us. After standing there for the longest time she had us climb up on the float so we'd be ready when they drove it into the parade. My dad said he was going to a diner to drink coffee and read the paper until the parade started. He hadn't worn a coat.

When he called good-bye to me he said, "Have fun, Stacey! See you after the parade. Remember, when you come down from the float stay with your group leader. I don't want you to get lost."

Yikes. I could already see how crowded the area was getting. There were dozens of bands that were gathering and warming up their instruments in Central Park. All of the floats were lining up on Central Park West and hordes of clowns were milling around everywhere. From where I sat on the float I had a bird's-eye view of the big balloons on the street next to the Museum of Natural History. They keep them from blowing away by throwing huge nets over them that were held down by weights. If you were in a helicopter looking down on Central Park West around the Museum of Natural History just before the parade started you'd think it was a big, complicated board game. I felt really small and really alone. At that moment I wished with all my heart that Laine was on the float with me.

Fortunately, in the following moment the woman from Macy's gave me a cup of hot chocolate and a big smile. "How are you doing?" she asked.

"Okay." Then before she could leave I asked, "Where's Cinderella?"

"She'll be here," she said. "The stars usually arrive at the last minute. That way I get to be nervous. But don't you be."

I was nervous, though. I just couldn't wait for the parade to begin. Everyone was getting jittery with excitement. I went over in my head what I would say to Cinderella. I'd tell her my name and ask her how she liked being a star.

At a little before nine o'clock a man with a bullhorn started a ten-second countdown. Cinderella still wasn't there. What if she didn't come? "Three, two, one." The first band stepped off and the parade began. The Spiderman balloon turned the corner onto Central Park West and everyone cheered. Everyone but me. Where was Cinderella?

Then suddenly she was coming up the steps of the float. I didn't see how she had arrived. If she came in a car it wasn't anywhere that I could see. She was like magic, standing in the middle of us girls. We all looked at one another and laughed and smiled and said things like, "She's here." "I was really worried." "She's beautiful." It was as if we were no longer a bunch of strangers on a float, but princesses at court. Our queen had arrived.

Cinderella was the most beautiful person I had ever seen. Her gown went all the way to the ground in billowing clouds of blue and white satin. On her wavy red hair she wore a gold crown dotted with multicolored gems. Cinderella!

Suddenly our float was moving. The woman from Macy's who was walking alongside it called to us, "Smile and wave, girls." I looked up at Cinderella to see that she was already doing that.

It was awesome to be on a float in the Thanksgiving Day parade. Everyone along the parade route was in a happy and festive mood. Some of them were on stepladders so they could see over the tops of the heads of the people in front of them. But on the float we were higher than even the stepladder people. The music for the *Cinderella* float rose up around us. And Cinderella just kept on smiling and waving. My only disappointment was that I hadn't gotten to speak to her. Well, I thought, at least we'll be on television together.

When we got to Herald Square it was like a big stage. People were sitting on bleachers as if they were at a ball game. And Macy's was all lit up with Christmas lights. Right away I saw the television cameras and lights. We brightened our smiles and waved our arms even harder.

But something was wrong. Cinderella wasn't waving. Both of her hands were on her head, holding onto her hair. Her crown had blown off and was about to fall to the ground. I leaned out over the edge of the float. By raising to my tiptoes I was able to grab it. As I handed the crown to Cinderella I saw that our float had moved past Macy's.

Cinderella said, "Thanks," and quickly put the crown back on her head. As she did, I could see wisps of black hair on her neck and I realized she was wearing a wig. A wig that had almost blown off during the Thanksgiving Day parade.

Our float turned the corner onto Thirty-fourth Street, and Cinderella and I went back to waving and smiling.

A few minutes later we were on Seventh Avenue where the parade breaks up. "Okay, kids," the woman from Macy's said. "You can get down now."

I looked at Cinderella. Even though I'd been on the float for over two hours I didn't want the parade to be over. Cinderella said, "You're the one who saved my crown, aren't you?"

I had wanted so badly to talk to her and now all I could do was nod. She took off the crown and handed it to me. "Have a nice Thanksgiving," she said. As she hopped off the float I replied, "Thank you. Have a nice Thanksgiving." But she was gone. I couldn't spot her in the crowd. She disappeared as magically as she appeared. But I had the crown.

CHAPTER 5

As Dad and I walked into the apartment, the warm sweet-spicy aroma of turkey and stuffing engulfed us.

"Wow," my dad said. "Does that ever smell good." My mom, aunt Beverly, uncle Lou, Jonathan, and Kirsten came to meet us. Everyone was talking at once.

"Did you see me? Did you see me?" I called above the din of greetings. "How'd I look? I can't wait to tell you what happened."

"How come you weren't on TV?" Kirsten said. "We watched and watched for you."

My mother was squatting down in front of me. "Are you okay?" she said. "When I didn't see you on television I was worried."

Not on television? How could that be? "I was right next to Cinderella," I said. "The whole time."

"Well we looked at that part of the tape over

and over. We saw Cinderella and five little girls, but not you."

I wanted to cry. I knew I should be happy that I got to be in the parade and that Cinderella gave me her crown. But I was suddenly tired and hungry and feeling weepy.

We all went right into the living room and my mom put on the tape of the parade at the moment when the Cinderella float comes into view. At first the float was so far away that you could barely see Cinderella. You certainly wouldn't know that one of those dots around her was Stacey McGill. Next, the screen was filled with close-ups of the hosts who were talking about the band from Louisiana that was just before our float. Then they announced that our float was coming into the square. That's when there was a good shot of Cinderella and *five* adorable little girls waving and smiling. Cinderella was waving with one hand and holding onto her hair with the other. My father played the sequence forward and backward slowly.

"See," Kirsten said. "You're not there, Stacey. Where were you?"

But I could see me. "There I am," I said.

"Where?" Jonathan asked.

"Play it back again," I said to my mom. I went over to the TV. The image of Cinderella holding onto her hair while the girls waved played in slow motion. I pointed to the sleeve of a navy blue coat on the edge of the screen. "That's me," I said.

I told them how I had saved Cinderella's crown, and I showed it to them. My mother said I had a very special souvenir and that I should take good care of it. I felt happy again as I placed it carefully over the corner of my bureau mirror.

The rest of vacation was fun. Laine was at her grandmother's in Pennsylvania for vacation so I couldn't play with her. But my mother and I went Christmas shopping on Friday. And Mom and Dad and I saw a movie on Saturday. Every once in awhile I'd remember that the kids at school had said they'd watch for me on TV, and I wasn't even on TV. I was worried that they wouldn't believe I had been *in* the Thanksgiving Day parade. That they would think I had made the whole thing up.

Sure enough. On Monday morning I hadn't even taken my coat off when Laine yelled from across the room, "Stacey, I didn't see you on TV." A bunch of other kids said the same thing. Everyone was calling out, "Where were you?" "I didn't see you." "How come you said you were going to be in the parade?"

Just then Miss Moss called us to order and we gathered around her for morning songs.

Then it was time for Show and Share. "Who'd like to begin?" she asked.

Before I could raise my hand and say "Me. I want to be first," Petey was standing in the middle of the circle holding up a wishbone. "I had the biggest turkey of the world," he said. "And I ate the whole thing."

All the kids were amazed by this, but Miss Moss turned the discussion into the size of other turkeys. No one had eaten a hundred-pound turkey like Petey (not even Petey), but the talk about turkey sizes went on for a very long time.

Finally Miss Moss said, "All right, you may sit down now, Petey. Who's next?"

I stood up and shouted, "Me," before anyone else. I went to the middle of the circle, took the crown out of my backpack, and told the story about how I saved Cinderella's crown. I didn't tell the kids that her hair was a wig because some of them probably still believed that it was the real Cinderella, just like some of them still believed in the Tooth Fairy.

Everyone was very impressed with the crown and wanted to hold it. Miss Moss asked me how I felt about handing it around the circle. I said, "Okay, if everyone's hands are clean." I was looking right at Petey holding that old wishbone when I said it.

Miss Moss suggested that Petey wash his hands. Then we passed my crown around the circle. I didn't mind anymore that I hadn't been on television. And finally my Cinderella story had a happy ending. That's why I said that sometimes when you think a story has an unhappy ending it's just that it isn't over yet.

WHEN I WAS EIGHT

CHAPTER 6

I grew up a lot in the three years between kindergarten and third grade. So did Laine. At least we thought we did.

By then we were X-tra best friends. We would say to one another, "You're my best friend." Or, "I won't go to that sleepover unless you're invited, too." And we both liked going to school. Mostly because it meant we were together all day. We were both pretty good at schoolwork, too, so being in classes didn't make us miserable like it does some kids.

Laine and I also played with one another on the weekends. The bummer was that since we weren't allowed to travel around the city alone we couldn't go the six blocks between our apartment buildings by ourselves.

In Stoneybrook even little kids are allowed to walk over to a friend's house on their own or to go for a ride on their bikes. In New York City that doesn't happen, at least not in the crowded neighborhoods of Manhattan. Most parents don't let their kids leave the apartment building without an adult until they're in about the seventh grade.

So on weekends our parents would accompany Laine or me to one another's apartments. Sometimes, if our parents were in a hurry, they'd let us take the elevator up by ourselves.

Here's a typical Saturday afternoon for Laine and me when we were eight years old. I remember this day particularly well.

It was after lunch and the doorman called on the intercom to tell me that Laine was coming up. I went out into the hall and waited in front of the elevator door for her. While I was waiting I turned my eyelids inside out. When the elevator doors opened and Laine saw me she shrieked with delight. It was the first time I'd done that. The boys in our class were always doing it, but I'd been too afraid to until I heard the elevator coming and wanted to surprise Laine.

"How'd it look?" I asked her when she finished cracking up.

"Very weird," she said. "Very neat."

I saw that her mother wasn't with her so I asked, "Did your dad drop you off?"

"Yeah. On his way to the theater. I wanted to ride my bike over but he said he had to bring me. It's ridiculous."

I said, "I know what you mean." As I checked in the hall mirror to see that my eyelids weren't all baggy from being stretched inside out, I said, "Parents are so overprotective. It's such a pain."

"It's like we have bodyguards," Laine said. "Who needs it?"

"Oh, well." I led the way into my apartment. "Let's go watch music videos on MTV."

We went to my room, punched on the TV, and played with my toys. Our favorite toy that year was this amazing ten-room Victorian dollhouse that my grandmother had given me for Christmas when I was six. It was the very best of my toys. I smile to myself when I remember playing with my dollhouse to a background of hard rock videos on MTV.

If a song we especially loved came on we'd stop playing with the dolls and get up to dance. Or we might lip-sync the lyrics for one another. Laine did a wild Madonna. I liked to be Sting, which cracked her up. When the song was over we would return to playing with the dollhouse.

After a long while of playing this way we were suffering from a hunger that only ice cream could satisfy. We knew the only exception to the "you-must-have-an-adult-with-you" rule was that we could go alone to the ice-cream store that was around the corner from my building.

We found my mother in the kitchen eating a snack. Good, I thought, she won't want to come with us. I said, "We want to go get ice cream. Okay?"

My mother looked at us thoughtfully. Even though she and Mrs. Cummings had agreed weeks before that we could go for ice cream alone, my mother always made us feel like it was the biggest deal in the world. "Well," she said reluctantly, "I guess it's all right. But don't dawdle," she added. "Come right back."

Laine asked, "Is it okay if we eat there, Mrs. McGill?" She gave my mother her most winning, innocent smile. "That way we'll be more alert when we're walking back."

"That's very good thinking, Laine," she said.

I said, "That ice cream store's been awful crowded lately. Hasn't it, Laine?"

Laine agreed. "We had to wait in a long line last time, so don't get worried if we're not back right away."

My mother handed us each a dollar. "Come home as quickly as you can. I'll worry until I see the whites of your eyes again."

Laine and I went down on the elevator and through the lobby. We said, "Hello, Mike," to the doorman and stepped out onto the sunny street.

One of my favorite New York City feelings is when I've been cooped up in the apartment all day and I go outside. The energy of the city charges through me like a surge of electricity. I feel taller and lighter and faster than I ever do indoors. That's the feeling I had that day when Laine and I held hands and happily ran all the way to the ice cream store.

There was no line so we got our cones right away and went back outside with them. Laine had her usual Swiss almond chocolate with chocolate sprinkles and I had vanilla with multicolored sprinkles. These were my sweet prediabetes days. If I'd known then that in four years I'd be told I couldn't eat sugar again, I'd have had double sprinkles! But that Saturday I was just a carefree eight-year-old who thought she'd be eating sprinkles for the rest of her life.

We were standing outside the store, leaning on the window and eating our cones, when I told Laine, "There are some neat things in a store on the next block."

"Show me," Laine answered.

Neither of us acknowledged that the store was in "you-may-not-go-alone" territory. We just walked and walked until we got to the store. It was a variety store that had a lot of playful stuff in the window. There was a shower curtain with a map of the world on it and slippers that looked like stuffed animals.

"I like the gumball machine best," I told Laine.

She pointed her ice-cream cone at a plastic

crayon that was taller than us and said, "My favorite is the big red crayon. And," she added with a grin, "I want a coloring book to go with it." We giggled because we knew there was no such thing. (It would have to be as big as that store window!)

As we talked and laughed like this, I watched our reflection in the window and thought we looked pretty grown-up.

Walking back to my apartment a few minutes later I said, "Let's pretend we live in our own apartment. Not with our parents."

"Let's," Laine agreed.

We talked about it all the way home. Opening the door to the apartment I still lived in with my parents, I called out, "Mom, we're back." When she came into the hall to greet us, Laine and I both had our eyelids inside out.

My mother said, "That's disgusting. I didn't know kids still did that."

Laine and I tried to tell her, "You said you wanted to see the whites of our eyes," but we were laughing so hard I don't think my mother heard us.

We ran to my room to talk some more about getting our own apartment. We decided that it would be a studio apartment. (A studio apartment is only one room, but has kitchen equipment and a bathroom.) There were three good reasons for getting a studio. One, it wouldn't be too expensive. Two, we wouldn't need a lot of furniture. And three, it would be easier to keep clean.

"I have an idea," I said. "Let's make a list of the stuff we'll need for it." I used my prettiest stationery and headed it, "For Our Apartment."

(In my memory box I found the list Laine and I made. I thought of sending it to Laine to remind her of what good friends we used to be, but we aren't friends anymore and I don't think she'd appreciate receiving it.)

Anyway, here's the list:

FOR OUR APARTMENT

2 forks
2 spoons
2 knives
2 dishes
2 bowls (for ice cream)
take-out menus from
Ray's Pizza
Hunan Palace
Burritoville
and Three Brothers
1 convertible couch
2 bean bag chairs
1 gumball machine
1 big red crayon

The day we made that list Laine called me as soon as she got home. "I thought of three more things to put on the list," she said. "Write them down."

I got out the list and a pen and went back to the phone. "Shoot," I said.

"Add: 'TV,' 'VCR,' and 'telephone.' "

"Why do we need a phone?" I asked. "We'll be living together so we don't need to call each other."

"Sta-cey," she said, "we need a phone to order take-out."

I laugh when I think of it now. But that weekend Laine and I were very serious about our plans. We vowed that we would save all of our gifts and allowance money from that day forward so we'd have enough money for our apartment. We figured by fifth grade, latest, we'd have convinced our parents we could live alone.

The next day I asked Laine, "What if the landlord asks why two kids are by themselves? What will we say?"

"We'll tell him that we're orphans and that we have a kind old grandmother who comes by every couple of days to check on us."

"Why aren't we living with our grandmother?" I asked.

Even Laine was stumped by that. But only

for a minute. She put her hands on her hips. "Because she lives in a nursing home, of course."

"And we'll say we're sisters," I added.

Laine and I smiled at one another. "Perfect," she said.

Sunday night while I was taking a bubble bath I thought of some other things to add to our apartment list: "bubble bath, soap, toothbrushes, toothpaste." I could hear my mother in her room talking on the phone, but I couldn't make out the words, just that she was talking to Mrs. Cummings.

While I was sitting there making a beard out of bubbles, my mother came into the bathroom and sat on the edge of the tub. "Well, Stacey," she said, "you and Laine are the luckiest girls in the world."

Was it possible that our parents had agreed that Laine and I could get our own place? How amazingly easy!

"Why are we lucky?" I asked.

"We've enrolled you both in the Beresford Ballroom Dance Academy," she said. "You begin on Tuesday."

"Ballroom dancing!" I shouted. "That's dorky and boring. Only babies do it." I couldn't believe Laine had agreed to this. "Does Laine know?"

My mother said that of course Laine knew. That it was her mother's idea. "Someday," my mother said, "you'll be grateful that you know ballroom dancing. It's a skill you'll use through your life. And you'll enjoy the classes, too."

"Fat chance," I mumbled.

After my bath I went into the living room to complain to my father. But he just said, "You're a big girl now, Boontsie. You can't stand on a guy's feet the way you used to do with me."

When I was little (and he called me 'Boontsie' *all* the time) I would stand on his feet and he would dance me around. But I hadn't done that in years.

"Laine and I do fast dances," I told him. "I want to learn how to moonwalk. Ballroom dancing is for babies and sissies."

"I beg to differ with you," my father said. He got up and changed the station on the radio from the classical station to a light music one. Then he walked over to my mother who was sitting on the couch and bowed. "May I have this dance?"

She smiled and got up. They danced around the room. I knew it was hopeless to argue with them that night. And it was too late to call Laine and plan a counterattack. So I went to bed.

Over the next two days Laine and I tried

pleading, sulking, and bribing. We even both promised we'd do all our homework before calling one another on the phone everyday. But nothing would change their minds.

My mother closed the discussion by saying, "We already paid. Six lessons won't kill you."

On Tuesday we had to wear "appropriate ballroom dancing attire" to school so we'd be ready for the four o'clock ballroom dancing class. The dress my mother decided was "appropriate" for ballroom dancing was a pink silk shift dress with a lace collar, white tights, and black patent leather shoes. I really loved that dress, but I never, ever would have worn it to school. So I wore my longest sweater over it and kept it on all day. Laine did the same thing to cover up her plaid satin dress.

Mrs. Cummings picked us up from school to take us across town for our ballroom dancing lesson. In the cab she told us, "Now, you two, be sure you take off your sweaters and, Laine, comb that hair of yours. And don't worry if your hands get sweaty when you dance with boys. That always happens at first. It's normal."

Boys! That was going to be the worst of it. And holding hands! How could we?

When we got out of the cab Mrs. Cummings leaned out the window and reminded us that my mother would be picking us up in an hour.

"Now hurry," she said. "I can tell you're daw-
dling. You don't want to be late on your first
day."

"Oh, yes we do," Laine mumbled as we
walked toward the building as slowly as we
dared.

When we got on the elevator to go to the
fifth floor I said, "I can't go through with it."

"Me either," Laine agreed.

"So let's not," I said as we got off the elevator. "Let's ditch it."

CHAPTER 7

As the elevator doors closed behind us we found ourselves face-to-face with an ornate gold-on-white sign: *Beresford Ballroom Dance Academy*. From behind the door we heard the kind of music we both thought was "sappy." Laine and I looked at one another. She said, "Okay. Let's ditch it."

Just then the academy door opened and a mother walked out. "Girls," she said. "You made it just in the nick of time. Hurry."

I said, "We don't go here."

"Of course you do," she said. "Look at those darling shoes and pretty white stockings. And shy is written all over your faces. Now go ahead. You'll have a wonderful time."

She was still holding the door open and gesturing for us to go in. The door closed behind us and we were standing alone in a small waiting area. To our right were two big windows that looked into the studio. Through the windows we saw twenty or so boys and girls nervously (and miserably) waiting for the class to begin. The music was coming from a piano where a young man sat with his back to us. The teacher, in a calf-length royal blue cocktail dress, was facing away from us, too. She was putting a pile of sheet music in front of the piano teacher.

We ducked down before she turned around to begin the class. Laine pulled my hand and whispered, "This way." We crawled on our hands and knees into a cloakroom that was no bigger than a large closet and sat on the floor to strategize.

We decided to take turns spying on the class. The first thing we needed to know was if the teacher took attendance.

Laine went first. In a few minutes she came back to report, "She didn't take attendance. I don't think she ever will."

It was my turn. I took a quick peek at the class and scurried back. "Laine, you're not going to believe who's in the class. Randal Peterson *the third*!" Randal was the snobbiest boy in our grade. He bragged that he was going to be a senator someday. And then president. If a teacher, or even another kid, didn't add "the third" when they said his full name he would correct them. Laine and I whispered to one another that Randal Peterson the third figured he better learn ballroom dance so he'd look good at his inaugural ball when he became president.

"President of jerks," Laine added.

Laine went to see if we knew anyone else in the class. "Samantha and Cecile," she reported. They were girls we knew who were so super proper that they always wore stockings to school. They hated us. Laine thought they were jealous, but I think we seemed as weird to them as they did to us.

"Are they dancing yet?" I asked.

"They're learning how to say hello to one another at a dance. It's *so* dorky."

We spent the rest of the class like that, sneaking peeks and giggling in the cloakroom.

It was my turn to watch when Mrs. Dandyworth announced that they'd have one more number. (Her name makes her sound old, but she's my mother's age, which wasn't very old then.) I crept back to Laine and whispered, "We better go."

On the elevator I told Laine that Randal Peterson the third was doing something called the box step with Samantha. Laine said, "Samantha could be the first lady *the third* someday." We giggled all the way down.

When my mother arrived we were waiting for her in the lobby. She said, "I'd hoped to get a glimpse of the class."

"You can't anyway," Laine said. "It's not allowed."

"I guess it would make you all shyer if parents watched," my mother said. The three of us were walking down the street toward Central Park. "I hope they have a recital at the end of the course."

"Sorry, Mom," I told her. "No recital."

"Take my hands," she directed as we stepped off the curb to cross Fifth Avenue. Laine and I exchanged an exasperated look behind her back as we each took one of her hands. She still treated us like babies.

Our next ballroom dancing class was on Friday. Laine and I had forgotten about having our own apartment. We were too busy strategizing our coverup for not going to ballroom dance class. We'd already told our mothers that "Appropriate Ballroom Dance Attire" included denim skirts. And they bought it.

"Well, you girls are the ones attending the class," Mrs. Cummings told Laine. "You should know."

When she dropped us off in front of the building for class, instead of going in we stood at the front door and waved good-bye to her. As the cab pulled away she was gesturing out the window for us to get going. We did. But not into the building. As soon as the cab was out of sight, Laine and I ran to the sidewalk and headed east.

We decided that if we spent ten minutes on each block we could walk the square block around the building and be back before my mother came to pick us up.

The next block was Madison Avenue. We went into a deli and got a pack of gum to split. Then we went into a stationery store that had toys, too. We played "I have this" for awhile. When the ten minutes we'd allocated for Madison Avenue were up we went back outside and walked around the corner. But Eighty-fifth Street wasn't very interesting. There were only brownstones with parking garages under them. So we retraced our steps to Madison Avenue and went back into that deli to get candy. Laine got Gummi Bears and I got Milk Duds.

We walked quickly back down Eighty-fifth Street to make up for the second visit to the Madison Avenue deli. We were out of breath when we turned onto our next street, which wasn't a street at all but an Avenue — Park Avenue. While Park Avenue is really wide and pretty, it's extremely boring to an eight-year-old. The only thing we could think of to do was count the hundreds of red tulips in the center strip that separates the cars that are going uptown from the cars that are going downtown.

When the ten minutes were up (and we'd counted 305 tulips) we turned the corner to walk the half block back to the front of the building where we were to meet my mother. By the time we got there we were laughing like crazy from the stories we made up about what was going on in the ballroom dancing class.

I said, "Samantha and Randal Peterson the third are doing the waltz with sweaty palms."

We were still laughing when my mother arrived a few minutes later.

"How was class?" she asked. "Did you have a good time?"

"Terrific," I said.

"When do we come again?" Laine asked.

My mother was in a great mood all the way home. "I just knew you girls would like it," she boasted.

I said, "I can't wait until Tuesday."

"Me either," Laine agreed.

When I think about it now I'm amazed that we got away with cutting our dance classes. But for the next two sessions that's what happened.

On Tuesday we were confident enough to go all the way to Lexington Avenue to get ice cream cones to eat while we window-shopped.

On Friday we took the same route, but this time went a little further to Second Avenue where we spent most of our time in a fancy children's bookstore. Then we went into a diner and sat at the counter and ordered Cokes.

And we still got back in plenty of time.

We'd discovered a happy solution to ballroom dance classes. Our parents thought we were taking ballroom dancing, which made them happy. We were not taking ballroom dancing, which made us happy.

"What'll we do today?" I asked Laine on Tuesday when her mother had pulled away in the cab.

"Let's go to FAO Schwarz," Laine answered.

"That's too far," I said. We were savvy New York kids and knew that FAO Schwarz (the best toy store in the world) was on Fifth Avenue at Fifty-eighth Street. We were near Fifth Avenue, but from Eighty-sixth to Fifty-eighth was two miles.

"We'll take the bus, of course," Laine said as she reached in her pocket. "I have four tokens." She opened her hand to show me. "We take the Fifth Avenue bus downtown. Let's go."

As the bus inched along we talked about the other times we'd been to FAO Schwarz and the wonderful toys we'd seen there. It was exciting to be going there on our own. After awhile I said, "This bus is slow."

"There's a lot of traffic lights," Laine replied.

I looked through the front window. "And traffic," I said. Just then a car horn honked as if to prove my point.

The bus crept along. "We're not going to have much time in the store," Laine said.

We started counting passengers. More people were getting on the bus than were getting off it and now there was standing room only, and not much of that. "I'm glad we got seats," I told Laine.

The briefcase belonging to a man standing over me hit me on the head. I slumped in my seat so it wouldn't happen again.

"I wonder what time it is," Laine said as she pushed up her sleeve to look at her watch. I looked at her watch too. It read ten minutes to five.

We stared at one another, our eyes big and scared. "Class is over in ten minutes," I told her.

"We're almost there," Laine said. She stood up to get a look out the window past the standing passengers. "It's the next stop, Stacey."

I stood up next to her. "It took us forty-five minutes to get this far. Even if we go back now we'll be thirty-five minutes late." (I told you I was good in math.)

"So let's go back," Laine said. At the next stop we got off the bus and crossed the street to wait for the bus going uptown. We stood there for five minutes before I realized that we were at the wrong bus stop. Fifth Avenue only goes downtown.

We ran all the way to Madison Avenue.

The only good luck we had that day was that a bus came right away. We hopped on, put our tokens in the meter, and joined the crush of passengers. My watch read 5:10. We were already ten minutes late.

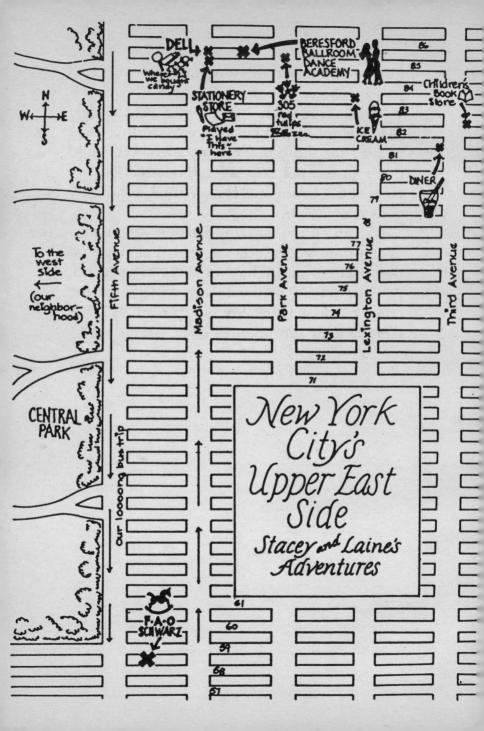

CHAPTER 8

Laine and I didn't say much during that slow, slow bus ride up to Eighty-sixth Street. We both kept checking our watches and feeling jittery. I silently prayed, "Please, bus, hurry. Please, bus, hurry." I didn't dare think what would happen when we got to our destination.

I checked my watch one last time as we ran the half block from the bus stop to the dance school. Five-thirty. We were half an hour late. And there was a police car parked outside.

We got on the elevator just as the doors were closing. "Hey there, young ladies," one of the other passengers cautioned. "You could get caught in the door that way."

I looked up to see that the speaker was a cop. So was the woman standing next to him. "What floor would you like, girls?" she asked.

"Five, please," Laine said in a weak un-Laine-like voice.

"Looks like we're all going to five," the police officer said.

They were smiling and friendly. I wondered how they would treat us when they found out we were the missing girls.

Laine and I took one another's hands. When the elevator door opened we were facing a crowd that started in the waiting room of the Beresford Ballroom Dance Academy and spilled out into the hall. There were students and their mothers, my mother, Mrs. Cummings, Mrs. Dandyworth, the piano player, and a bunch of other people, including uniformed security guards from the building.

Mrs. Dandyworth said, "The police are here."

"Stacey!" my mother shrieked.

"Laine!" Mrs. Cummings shouted. "Oh, thank heaven."

"I've never seen these girls before," Mrs. Dandyworth said.

Laine and I stood close together as we exited the elevator but our mothers yanked us apart.

It was one of those confusing but happy scenes like at the end of a lot of movies. Our mothers were hugging us, and they were happy because we hadn't been kidnapped. Mrs. Dandyworth was happy because it wasn't her fault that we were missing. The cops were happy because this was a case that wouldn't end with mounds of paperwork. And Samantha, Cecile, and Randal Peterson the third were thrilled because they had a great story to tell about us in school the next day.

Everyone was happy except Laine and me.

The first sign of big trouble was when we walked out of the building a few minutes later and our mothers decided to take us home in separate cabs.

"Let's keep them apart for awhile," my mother suggested.

"I couldn't agree more," Mrs. Cummings said. "But, please Maureen, let's not let this ruin our friendship."

"Don't worry, Peg. I'll call you tonight."

Laine and I exchanged woeful glances. That's when I wanted to cry.

"It was my fault," I told my mother on the way home. "It was all my idea. Don't let Mrs. Cummings punish Laine."

Later I learned that Laine had said the same thing to her mother. You can see why we were such good friends.

At home that night my parents interrogated me. I had to tell them everything we had done when we didn't go to dance class.

My father was most upset by the idea that I had lied to them.

"I didn't," I protested. "You never asked me if I was *going* to the class. You just asked if I had a good time, and" (my voice got smaller here) "I did."

"You knew what we meant by our questions, Anastasia," my father said. "What you did was deceitful. I'm very disappointed in you. How will we ever be able to trust you again?"

I was in much deeper trouble than I ever could have dreamed of. I said, "If I'd known you would find out, I wouldn't have done it."

"You're missing the point," my father said.

And they gave me the lecture about lying again. When I think about that incident from their point of view I can understand why they were upset. And now that I'm older and more experienced I have a much better understanding of why you shouldn't twist the truth around, especially when you're dealing with people you love. But then I could only see it from my point of view. And from my point of view, the punishment that my parents and Laine's parents had agreed on was awful.

"You and Laine cannot talk on the phone to one another for the next six weeks," my mother began.

"On weekends and after school you won't be allowed to play together either," my father continued.

It was my mother's turn again. "But you

and Laine will be together two afternoons a week to take a six-week course in ballroom dancing. Only this time we'll walk you right into the studio and pick you up in the waiting room. No more of this, 'Meet us in the lobby' business."

It was a long six weeks. And I never did like the ballroom dancing. I had sweaty hands to the very last dance, especially the day of the recital for our parents. (There was one.) And wouldn't you know that I almost always ended up dancing with boys who had sweaty hands, too.

The young ladies and gentlemen of the
Beresford Ballroom Dance Academy
cordially invite you to attend
a performance of ballroom dancing.
Tuesday, May 15
4:00 p.m.
Beresford Ballroom Dance Academy
35 East 86th Street, Fifth floor
New York City

Appropriate attire requested.

Well, my parents enjoyed it....

The only good thing about those classes was that when they ended Laine and I could go back to being best friends who could talk on the phone and play at each other's houses on weekends.

Believe it or not, now I'm glad I took ballroom dancing. I actually learned how to be coordinated. And if a guy knows something like the fox-trot or the lindy I don't step all over his toes. It's especially handy when I go to weddings or bar mitzvahs and someone like my father or uncle Lou wants to dance with me.

I think one of the reasons I chose this incident to include in my autobiography is because when it happened I was exactly the age that my favorite baby-sitting charge, Charlotte Johanssen, is now. Charlotte is an only child like me and we love one another like sisters. But still, she's a little kid. So when I think of what Laine and I did, and try to imagine how I'd feel if I were responsible for Charlotte and she did something like that . . . well, I get goose bumps all over.

Still, I learned a lot on those afternoons when we skipped classes. Being self-confident and independent during those hours of freedom proved to me that I wasn't afraid of new situations. And since I've had so many of these

Randal Peterson the Third and me
doing the sweaty palm waltz.

in my life (remember the two "Ds"), you can see that it's been helpful.

Sometimes, when I'm baby-sitting for elementary school kids, I try to remember how grown-up I already felt when I was eight years old. That way I won't treat them like babies.

Even though Laine and I aren't friends anymore I'm glad we were friends then. We had some great adventures.

WHEN I WAS TEN

CHAPTER 9

For three summers in a row our family had taken a vacation together in August. When I was seven we went to a dude ranch. The next summer we took a neat trip with Laine and her parents to San Francisco. And when I was nine we went to Ireland and Scotland. These were wonderful vacations with lots of activities and fun-filled things for us to do. But when I was ten my parents made a vacation decision that I couldn't believe.

They broke the news to me on a hot night in July. We were eating Chinese take-out at the kitchen table. Unaware that my parents were about to depress me, I was innocently eyeing the container of sesame noodles. I was hoping my mother would skip them and go right from her wonton soup to the chicken with snow peas so I could have a second helping of those noodles.

"So, Boontsie," my father said, "we've decided where we're going for vacation next month."

"Where?" I asked. I was hoping I was finally going to get to go to Disney World or that we'd go back to Ireland.

My mother said, "We've rented a house on an island in Maine for two weeks. You'll love it."

"On an island?" I said. "Oh, goody. A resort." I was remembering a winter vacation we took at a resort on the island of St. Thomas. I was already imagining myself snorkling, taking tennis lessons, and eating candlelit meals in fancy restaurants. My white sundress with the little blue flowers would be perfect.

My mother said, "There're no resorts on Pine Island. Just a few fishermen and their families. That's its charm. There's not much of anything there."

I stopped worrying about sesame noodles. "What do you mean 'there's not much of anything there'?"

"Your father's been working so hard," my mother said, "that I thought the best vacation for him would be to go to a place where he could do nothing but relax."

"What do you mean 'do nothing'?" I was getting nervous.

"We'll have a house in the woods," she said. "And there's the ocean."

"So there's a beach," I said. "People go to the beach and snorkle and stuff."

"It's not that kind of a beach," my father said.

When you think of beaches you think, "sand" right? Well, the place my parents had picked for a two-week vacation had a *rocky* beach. "Besides," my mother added, "the island's pretty far north so the water will be cold."

"But it's beautiful," my father added.

So, I told myself, forget the beach. I was still trying to make sense of their vacation choice and I wanted to be helpful, so I said, "Probably the only thing to do at night will be go to movies. We should stop going to movies in New York so we won't have seen everything when we get there."

"There isn't a movie theater on Pine Island,"

my father said. He was smiling.

"Or restaurants," my mother added. "That's how quiet it is." She was so delighted by this fact that she let out a little laugh.

Happy that there weren't any restaurants or movie theaters? They were acting incredibly weird.

My mother went on, "There isn't even a grocery store."

"What's so great about *that*?" I asked. "No restaurants or grocery stores means no food. What are we going to eat?" Were we going to spend two whole weeks playing *Swiss Family Robinson*?

"We'll shop on the mainland and bring it over in a motorboat," my mother said.

"What if we forget something?" I asked.

"Then we'll just have to do without," she answered. It *was* going to be like the *Swiss Family Robinson*.

My mother shoved the container of noodles in my direction. "Stacey, honey," she said, "I don't want sesame noodles tonight. Why don't you finish them?"

I looked down at my plate. It was empty. I'd been eating without knowing it. "Sure," I said. "Why not? It may be the last food I eat." I poked my chopsticks into the sesame noodles and dragged them onto my plate.

My father laughed. "Don't be so dramatic, Anastasia. You'll have a wonderful time. There's bound to be someone your age on the island for you to play with."

Someone? I thought. One person? What if I didn't like her? What if that one person was a *him*?

I spent the next two weeks before this so-called vacation being grumpy about it. Laine, who'd just come back from a vacation in *Paris* with her parents, was totally sympathetic. Most of my other friends were at sleepaway camp, so Laine and I would talk about the exciting time she'd had in Paris and the boring time I would have in Maine.

Meanwhile my parents couldn't have been happier.

My father went to a bookstore and picked out a bunch of paperback spy thrillers to read. He also said that maybe he'd do a little fishing.

My mother stocked up on her favorite staples, such as olive oil, honey mustard, and balsamic vinegar from Zabar's. She even bought two pie tins. "It's blueberry season in Maine," she explained. "I'll make homemade pies." My mother *never* made pies. Nobody I knew made pies. If we wanted pie we went to a bakery and bought one.

"What'll I do?" I asked.

"You can help me cook," my mother said. "This would be a perfect time for you to learn how."

"And maybe you'll want to do a little fishing with me," my father added.

I ran to my room and called Laine with the latest update on my parents' madness. "He's going to fish," I said. "You know, catch innocent fish with hooks and everything. And she and I are going to cook the fish."

"I wonder who's going to cut off their heads and clean out their guts?" Laine said.

"Not me," I told her. "I'm not going anywhere near those fish."

"Go see what they're talking about now," she suggested.

"Okay," I said. "You wait. Don't hang up and I won't hang up. I'll be right back."

I snuck into the hall, listened to my parents for a minute, then ran back to the phone. "They're talking about lobsters," I told her. "They said it would be great to eat lobster all the time. I don't even like lobster."

"Lobster is what Maine is famous for," Laine said. "And they're not hard to cook. You don't even have to kill them. You just throw them live into boiling water. When the shell turns red they're cooked. Oh, yeah, and you don't have to take their guts out until you eat them. Some people think the guts are delicious. I watched my dad eat them once. They're this pukey shade of green."

"Ew-ww! They put them *live* in boiling water and eat their guts? My parents are turning into cannibals."

"Bring a lot of books," Laine advised. "And be prepared to be b-o-r-e-d."

That night Laine asked her mother if I could stay with them while my parents went on vacation. She said no.

Two weeks later my parents and I got up at five-thirty in the morning to get an early start on the eight-hour drive to Maine. My mother brought along a separate suitcase just for the stuff she bought at Zabar's.

I had followed her example and gotten a two-week supply of candy and apricot rolls. In those days I depended on apricot rolls to get me through the day. There were twenty-eight of them in my suitcase. Two for each day. I imagined myself sitting under a tree being so bored that I had nothing to think about but when I'd have my next apricot roll.

My father came into my room. "Let's go, Stacey," he said. "We want to get an early start."

He was carrying his briefcase. "Hey, Dad,"

I said, "did you forget we're going on vacation?"

He whispered, "I have a little project for work that I've got to do. But let's keep it a secret from your mother for now. Can I put my briefcase in your suitcase?"

"Sure," I whispered back. "If it'll fit."

He seemed relieved that I agreed. He opened my suitcase. "Let me see what we can do here," he said as he moved my candy and apricot rolls from the top of the suitcase into the corners. "You'll want to put that candy in a container when we get there," he told me. "We don't want to have an infestation of ants in our house. Or raccoons. Skunks like candy, too."

"You're teasing me, Dad," I said. "And I don't think it's funny. I'm not in the mood."

"I'm not teasing you," he said. "I told you we're going back to nature." He patted me on the head. "Lighten up, Boontsie, it's a vacation."

The pat on the head reminded me that I hadn't packed my barrettes, headbands, and ribbons. "I forgot a few things," I told him. "But you can close my suitcase. I'll put them in my backpack."

As I took long twists of ribbons out of my drawer another question about the island popped into my head. "Dad," I asked, "are there snakes on that island?"

"I suppose," he said. "But they're probably not poisonous."

"*Probably* not poisonous?" Didn't my parents even care about my safety anymore?

My dad said, "Come sit on this suitcase, will you?" With my weight he was finally able to close it. It was stuffed to the gills with my favorite clothes, books, and toys. I was even taking an old Barbie doll that I'd lost interest in and some of *her* clothes. And of course I had my teddy bear, Goobaw. And my father's briefcase.

By six-thirty we were in the car and ready to roll. As we drove past Laine's block I thought, Good-bye, Laine.

Then we passed my favorite restaurant. I thought, Good-bye, restaurants.

Good-bye, movie theaters.

Good-bye, pizza parlors.

Then it was, Good-bye, New York City.

My parents took turns driving. During my mother's turn my father took a nap. She caught my eye in the rearview mirror and whispered, "See how relaxed he is already? Two weeks without work is going to make your father a new man." I guess they were already having problems in their marriage and she was wishing he'd change. I was wishing that I didn't know he'd brought his briefcase.

Five boring hours later I said good-bye to highways. The farther north we got the more uncivilized things became. Pretty soon there weren't even any decent radio stations.

Whoever had rented us the house told my father where the last supermarket was so we could get our groceries in a decent-sized store. It took a whole hour to buy what we'd need for two weeks.

Then it was another half-hour drive on curvy dirt back roads before we got to the shore. When we were finally at the dock where we'd get a boat to take us to the island, my father said, "Too bad it's not a nicer day."

"It'll clear up tomorrow," my mother said. "I think it's beautiful just like this."

Boy, I wondered, is she going crazy? The weather was lousy. It was cloudy and damp — and even though it was August, I felt cold.

We went into this garage near the shore to hire someone to take us to the island. I never thought all our stuff would fit on that boat. But Mr. Stanley (he's the guy who owned the boat) said, "It'll fit in her. Don't you worry, miss."

It wasn't the most relaxing boat ride. The water was choppy and it took forever. But, I thought, boats and water. If I could learn to water ski the vacation wouldn't be wasted. I tapped my dad on the shoulder to get his attention. "Is this the boat we're renting?" I had to yell it twice to be heard over the roar of the motor.

"We're not renting a boat," he yelled back. "Mr. Stanley will come get us at the end of the two weeks."

We weren't going to leave the island for two weeks? As we were *chop-chopping* over the water I could see the island from one end to the other. It wasn't very big. It was small. And my parents hadn't exaggerated about how few people lived there. When we were unloading our suitcases and groceries onto the dock in front of the house we were staying in, Mr. Stanley told me there were only three families on Pine Island. I told him that more people lived on one floor of my New York apartment building than on that whole island.

He said, "All nice folks here. But it is pretty quiet for the young ones. I guess there's one girl your age. That O'Connell girl."

After all our stuff was on the dock he got back in his boat to return to the mainland. As he roared away he turned and gave me a smile and a wave. No wonder he's smiling, I thought. He gets to leave.

I waved back, but I definitely was not smiling.

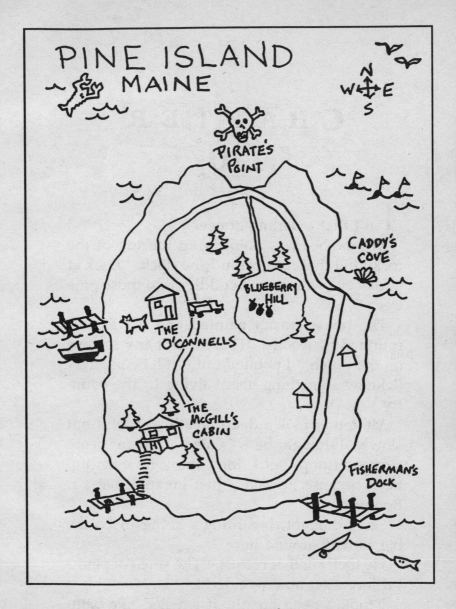

PINE ISLAND
MAINE

PIRATE'S POINT

CADDY'S COVE

BLUEBERRY HILL

THE O'CONNELLS

THE McGILL'S CABIN

FISHERMAN'S DOCK

What would I do for two weeks
on this very small island?

CHAPTER 10

"Isn't that a darling house?"

My mother was pointing to the top of the rocky hill that rose behind the dock. "Look at it, Stacey — the way it cuddles into those pine trees."

The house wasn't painted and it was surrounded by woods. "There aren't any screens on the porch," I pointed out. "It'll be buggy." (I knew something about living in the country.)

My father took a deep breath and let it out slowly. I thought he was mad at me for being such a grump, but I don't think he even noticed because he said, "Just breathe that air, Boontsie."

So, I thought, breathing's going to be the big activity around here.

He took another breath. "The smell of pines. I'd forgotten how wonderful it is."

I took a deep breath. It smelled like bathroom deodorant to me. What was so wonderful about that?

I soon learned there was another activity on the island besides breathing. We had to carry all our stuff up seventy-three rickety steps to the house. It took three trips.

By the time we got our luggage and groceries in the house and unpacked it all, it was already getting dark out. "I guess we'll wait until tomorrow to explore the island," my dad said.

Right, I thought, exploring rocks and trees should be thrilling. Then what do we do? Bake pies?

I walked around the house.

"Isn't it a darling place?" my mother said. "I knew you'd love it."

"I'm looking for the phone," I told her. "I've got to call Laine. I promised."

My father said, "We're roughing it, Stacey. There aren't any phones out here."

"No phones! Then we're totally cut off from civilization. That's horrible! It's dangerous! What if we get bitten by a snake or something?"

"Well, we're not alone on the island, Anastasia," my father said. "There are three other families."

"Unless they're smart and went someplace else for *their* vacation," I said.

* * *

The next morning I woke up to the sound
of the ocean crashing on the rocks. At first I
thought it was the crosstown bus needing a
new muffler. But then I opened my eyes and
saw a pine ceiling a foot from my face. When
I reached over the side of the bed and couldn't
feel the floor, I got the whole picture. I was
on the top bunk in a small bedroom in a small
cabin on a small island.

The inside walls of the cabin were made of
thin panels of wood, so in addition to the
ocean I could hear my father's raspy deep
sleep breathing and my mother's little snores.
With all that racket I couldn't get back to sleep.
So I got up to take a tour of the *cabin* in the
early morning light. (Forget "house," it definitely was a cabin.)

The kitchen, dining area, and living area
were all in one room. A counter separated the
kitchen from the rest of the room. In that section there was a round table with four chairs,
a couch, and two armchairs. The chairs were
pretty comfortable to sit in, but if you looked
under the bedspreads that covered them you'd
see that the upholstery was ratty.

I was pretty interested in the porch, so I
went out there. The breeze off the ocean surprised me. It smelled salty and cool and (I had
to admit) it did have a nice clean pine smell

that beat bathroom deodorant by a mile.

But what was in the woods that surrounded us on three sides? And where were the snakes? Did they hang from trees and slither down onto your head? Or were they creeping along the forest floor waiting for a chance to curl around your leg and strike? And what about bears?

An arm went around my shoulder. I screamed and jumped about a mile in the air.

"Sorry if I scared you," my mother said. She was looking out to the ocean and doing that deep breathing again. "Isn't it beautiful, Stacey? I can't believe we're really here."

"I believe it," I said.

I went inside to get dressed. There wasn't a closet in my "room," so I'd stacked all of my clothes on the bottom bunk. I dressed in my thickest pair of jeans, my red high-top sneakers, and a long-sleeved blue polo shirt. Over that I'd wear my white denim jacket. I was glad I'd brought my wide-brimmed straw hat with the red checked bow. That would protect my head. *Nothing* was going to bite me.

Back in the kitchen-etc. room my parents were making breakfast and oohing and ahhing about the great night's sleep they'd had.

While they were enjoying their breakfast I watched nervously as my father buttered himself a fourth piece of toast. If he did that every day we'd run out of bread and butter in no time.

After breakfast I told my parents I was going for a walk. They seemed pleased that I was enthusiastic enough to go exploring on my own. That surprised me because in New York City they wouldn't let me go half a block by myself. Weren't they even a little concerned for my safety?

"Be back by noon," my mother said.

My father said, "If you stick to the dirt road that starts behind our house you won't get lost. That's the only road and it circles the island."

I went to the road, which was more like a path. I made sure to walk right in the middle so I was as far away as possible from the towering pine trees. As I walked along I got glimpses and sometimes big views of the rock ledge and the ocean beyond that. There was no denying that it was beautiful. And I really liked the salt air.

I hadn't gone far when I saw a house. There were chickens running loose in the yard. As I got closer a dog pushed out through the screen door and stood in the yard with its head up in the air barking at me. I stopped to consider my options. I could retrace my steps and start over in the other direction. But since the road was a circle, sooner or later I'd have to pass that house and that dog. I wasn't going to make the island any smaller for myself by cutting off one major section of it.

"Tippy! Come here, Tippy." A girl came out of the house. The dog ran back to her. I took a few steps closer.

"Hi," I called. "Is your dog friendly?"

"Yeah," she replied. "Sure."

I was going to keep on walking, when I thought, use your head, Stacey. This could be the only other kid on the whole island and two weeks is a very long time in such a small place without anyone to play with.

I pointed in the direction I'd come from and said, "I'm staying in the cabin over there."

The girl and the dog were walking toward me. The girl said, "You must be the kid staying in the Andersons' cabin."

"How'd you know?" I asked. As I reflect on it, this is not the nicest way to introduce yourself to someone new, but she answered me anyway.

"Mr. Stanley told me."

"Oh-hh," I said. "I think he told me about you, too."

About then, with this red-haired, freckle-faced girl grinning at me, and her brown mutt of a dog happily wagging its tail, my manners came back. "I'm Stacey McGill," I said.

"I'm Mara O'Connell," she answered. "I was just going over to your place to see if you wanted to go blueberry picking with me. The blueberries are really good this year."

"Yeah," I said. "Sure. There isn't much else to do around here."

"I'll get us some buckets," she said.

As we continued down the road swinging our empty buckets Mara didn't talk much. That surprised me. Since there couldn't be any kids for her to play with you'd think she'd have been yakking a mile a minute.

I broke the silence by saying, "I can't believe there aren't any phones here. I was supposed to call my best friend Laine as soon as I got here. We talk on the phone all the time. How can you live without a phone?"

"It's no big deal," Mara said. "We have a two-way radio." She said it in a cold way that kept me from asking how a two-way radio worked.

"So do you stay here all summer?" I asked. "It must be so boring."

"I live here all year round," she said. "I've lived on this island all my life."

"Oh," I said. "Well, what about school?"

"My brother and I take the boat to school on the mainland," she said. "Unless the weather's really terrible. Then we use the two-way to get our assignments."

I was still absorbing the idea that she'd lived her whole life, even winters, on the island, when we made a turn that brought us to the end of the land. We were standing on a rock ledge facing open ocean on three sides.

Mara looked out and let the wind whip her hair. I held on tight to my hat. "This is Pirate's Point," she said.

Instead of saying, "Wow, it's beautiful," or "How come they call it Pirate's Point?" I said, "How big is this island anyway?"

Mara ignored my question and said to follow her if I wanted to pick blueberries. We took a path so narrow that we had to go single file. I got spooked on that trail. I thought a snake had landed on my hat when it was just a tree branch that hit it. Wide-brimmed straw hats aren't too cool for hiking in the woods.

We climbed up and up through those woods until we came to a clearing. Mara said, "This is Blueberry Hill."

I was so grateful to be out of the woods that I said, "It's nice."

I copied what Mara did when she bent down in the middle of the low shrubbery that covered the clearing and started picking blueberries. As we picked and ate I asked her again, "How big is this island anyway?"

"Three-quarters of a mile long and a third of a mile wide," she said.

I did some quick math in my head and told Mara, "That's only fifteen New York City blocks long by six or seven city blocks wide. You've spent your whole life in a space that goes from Seventieth Street to Eighty-fifth Street and from, say, Riverside Drive to Central Park West. Now that I think about it, Central Park is a lot bigger than your whole island."

"So?" she said. "What's that supposed to mean?"

"It means that you live in an incredibly small place."

"So what if it's small? There isn't any crime here, is there? Or homeless people. Or who-knows-what-all that happens in big cities. No pollution either. I like it here."

I had a feeling that Mara wasn't too thrilled with me. I wasn't too thrilled with her either. It was pretty clear that we had nothing in common.

When we were walking back with our buckets of blueberries I tried to get the conversation going again by asking her, "What do you do around here? I mean really."

Mara had that cold note in her voice again, but she told me anyway. "I fish with my father and brother sometimes. I take care of my little sister. And the chickens are my responsibility."

"But what do you do for fun?"

"Just living here is fun," she said. "You came here for vacation, didn't you?"

"It wasn't my idea. My parents dragged me here. I wanted to go back to Ireland."

I noticed her eyes light up when I said "Ireland," but she didn't ask me anything about it.

"And," she said, "I check the lobster traps. That can be fun."

"Do you eat the lobsters?"

"Sure. We could have a lobster for lunch. We could cook it outside. That's fun."

"You cook them while they're still alive, don't you?"

"Of course. That's the way it's done. They die instantly." She gave me that cold look again. "You're not one of those city people who gets all sensitive about the poor lobsters, are you?"

"Why shouldn't I be?" I asked. "How would you like to be thrown into boiling water?"

"If people didn't eat lobsters my father wouldn't make a living."

"I just can't say I approve of it, that's all." We'd reached her house. "Anyway," I said, "I have to go. I told my mother I'd be home by lunch."

I handed Mara the bucket of berries I'd picked. "Thanks," I said. "It was fun."

"You can have them. You picked them, didn't you?" She was glaring at me. "Or are you afraid you'll hurt them? After all, they're alive."

"That's different," I said. I turned and walked off without saying good-bye.

My parents were grilling hamburgers outside and had set a little table on the porch for lunch. They were delighted that I had met a girl my age and went on and on about the blueberries I picked. My mother dished them into white bowls and said we'd eat them with cream for dessert.

While we were eating, Mom and Dad asked me lots of questions about Mara and her family. I told them I thought it was disgusting to make your living capturing innocent lobsters. My mother asked me how I thought a cow got to be hamburgers. And my father said, "I just hope we can buy our lobsters directly from the O'Connells."

At that moment I saw Mara coming toward our house. We all got up and went into the yard to meet her. She was carrying a bucket that she placed on the ground in front of us, saying, "My father said to give these to you." We all looked in the bucket where three *huge* lobsters tried to move around in that cramped space. I was the only one in my family who didn't say thank you.

The first day of our fun-filled
family vacation on Pine Island, Maine.

My father offered Mara a hamburger, but she said she'd already eaten. My mother asked her if sometime she would give us a tour of the island. She said, "Sure. I could do it now."

My father said, "Maybe we could do it tomorrow. I'd hoped to do some — " He stopped abruptly, but my mother finished the sentence for him.

"Work," she said. "I know that you brought your briefcase, Ed — after you promised me you wouldn't work during our vacation."

My father, seeing that Mara and I were just standing there watching them, said, "You know what, Mara, I think this afternoon would be just perfect."

Mara seemed to like my parents a lot more than she liked me. She smiled and talked a blue streak while we traipsed behind her. She pointed out this field and that cove and told us who lived where. We heard about the worst hurricane, the biggest snowstorm, and the best lobster season. I was definitely b-o-r-e-d. But my parents loved the tour and seemed to have made up, at least for the moment. I thought, Maybe I can go back to New York and *Mara* can live with Mom and Dad for the next two weeks. Not just because I was bored but because I was suddenly afraid that my parents would spend the next twelve days arguing about my father and his work.

When we got back, Mara said she had to go home to clean out the chicken coop, and asked me if I wanted to help. I said, "No thanks."

"Too messy for you?" she asked. There was that cold look again.

"I've got to write to Laine since I can't call her," I replied.

Mara jumped off the porch and said, "Maybe I'll see you tomorrow."

Fat chance, I thought.

The next morning my parents announced that we were going to spend the day in Caddy's Cove on the other side of the island. Their big plan was to dig for clams, lie on the rocks, and eat a picnic lunch of the lobster salad they'd made with the lobster I hadn't eaten the night before. When I said I didn't want to go, they just said, "Okay. Do whatever you want."

So an hour or so later when Mara showed up I didn't have much choice but to hang out with her. I showed her around the cabin, which of course she'd been in before. We played checkers on the porch and I kept asking her things such as if she'd ever been on a subway or an escalator and if she'd seen this movie and that movie. Since the movie theater closest to Pine Island was a boat ride and a twenty-mile drive away, Mara didn't see many movies. She didn't even have a VCR.

She asked me things such as whether I'd ever eaten a raw egg or driven a truck and how could I think I was such a big shot if I was afraid to sleep on Blueberry Hill alone at night. Sleeping outdoors without even a tent over her head was Mara's idea of a thrill. I couldn't imagine being brave enough to do that. But I didn't let her know I thought she was brave.

And even though I knew she was dying to know all about my trip to Ireland I wasn't going to tell her a thing about it unless she asked.

We played five games of checkers and Mara won four of them. Instead of saying she was a good player I said, "I guess since there's nothing to do around here you play a lot of checkers."

She ignored my comment and suggested we hike the rocks around the island. She said we'd start on the rock ledge in front of the cabin and climb the ledge around the whole island until we got back where we started.

Here's why I wasn't about to do it. If you

slipped (or were pushed), you'd fall hundreds of feet into the crashing surf. Fun, huh?

I said, "Let's play with my Barbie doll."

I could tell that Mara was impressed with all the outfits I had for Barbie and that she liked playing with her. But she never said so.

The next day was cloudy and drizzly, so my mother was going to cook and my father was going to take out his briefcase. When I heard them start to argue about that I decided to bring my Barbie doll to Mara's house. I was surprised to find that Mara was alone with her little sister. Alice was this cute one-year-old who was just learning to walk. I liked her better than Mara. So I played with Alice, and Mara played with my Barbie doll.

I couldn't get over it. While Mara's mother and father were fishing they trusted her with the baby. I didn't know any other ten-year-olds who got to baby-sit like that. I pretended that I was the one who was responsible for Alice, which was a lot of fun.

Mara and I weren't talking much, but after I'd put Alice down for her nap, Mara asked me, "Want to sleep out tonight? We don't have to go far from the house if you're afraid."

"I'm not afraid and I don't want to sleep out," I said. "I think it's stupid to sleep outdoors if you can be in a comfortable bed."

"You're just a snob," replied Mara.

"Well, you're just a hick," I shot back. "So stay away from me, okay?"

"No problem."

I stormed out of the house and ran all the way back to the cabin.

CHAPTER 11

By the time I got to the cabin I was so filled with angry thoughts and feelings toward Mara, and toward my parents for bringing me to Pine Island, that I thought I'd burst. But I was quickly distracted from my anger. As I stepped onto the porch I heard this huge crash, and a scream from my father. I couldn't get inside fast enough.

My mother and I reached Dad at the same time. He'd fallen off a step stool and was lying on the floor. "Ouch," he said. "Oh-hh, it hurts. Help me up."

My mother told him to wait and not try to stand. "It's my ankle," he said. "I was trying to get a book from the top shelf." I knew right away that he slipped off the step stool because he'd climbed it in stocking feet. When I was taking care of Alice I took off her socks so she wouldn't slip all over when she tried to walk.

Even through my dad's socks I could see that his ankle was getting puffy.

My mother said, "It must be sprained."

"I've had sprains before," he said. He grimaced in pain and I noticed how pale he was getting. "I think this time it's broken."

"Quick, Stacey," my mother said. "Run to the O'Connells' and see if Mara's mother or father can take us over to the mainland. We've got to get your father to a hospital."

I was so frightened that I was halfway to Mara's before I remembered that her parents weren't home. But I figured she'd know someone else who could take us to the mainland, so I kept going.

I spilled out my news and asked who could take us. "Me," Mara said. "I can take him in the motorboat."

"You can drive a motorboat?"

"Sure," she said. Then she mimicked me, "What else is there to do around here?"

I didn't care that she'd thrown that in my face. I was just glad someone could help my father. "You wake up Alice," Mara said. "Her life jacket is hanging next to the kitchen door. Bring three adult-sized ones for you guys. I'll drive the boat over to your dock."

"How can I carry the life jackets and Alice?" I asked.

"Oh, right. I forgot you can't drive. I was

thinking you'd take the pickup." By then Mara was in the kitchen. I was right behind her. In an instant, she was out the door, loaded down with life jackets.

I tried to imitate her efficient manner by remembering to grab extra diapers and bottles of juice and milk for Alice.

By the time I got to our cabin Mara had tied her motorboat to the dock and was running up the steps. That's when I thought, how are we ever going to get my father down those stairs? But Mara had already figured it out.

"I'll get the pickup truck," she said, "and Mrs. McGill, you can help Mr. McGill into it and drive it over to the fisherman's dock. There aren't any steps there. I'll meet you with the boat."

My parents were amazed by Mara. So was I.

While Mara was getting the pickup my mother and I decided that I should stay behind with Alice until her mother got back. Since it was only for an hour even my mother thought it was okay for me to take care of Alice by myself. (That was my very first baby-sitting job.) Mara reminded me to take Alice to her house before her parents got back and to tell them everything that had happened.

Alice padded around behind me while I

straightened up the mess from my father's fall and did the lunch dishes. Then I changed her diaper and we went back to her house.

Mr. and Mrs. O'Connell were nice, but they didn't seem to think it was any big deal that Mara knew what to do in an emergency. Her father used the two-way radio to call the hospital. (I finally saw how one worked.) When he got off he told me that my father had broken his ankle. He'd have to wear a cast and use crutches for a couple of weeks, but then he'd be fine. They'd just left the hospital.

I said I'd go home and wait for my parents, but the O'Connells insisted that I stay with them, and that the two families would have dinner together that night.

I helped Mrs. O'Connell make a blueberry pie while Mr. O'Connell cleaned some fish for the main course. (That fish was the most delicious thing I've ever eaten. The pie was pretty amazing, too.)

I guess you can figure out that things between Mara and me smoothed out after that. She was a first-class hero in my book. And a very nice person. Nice enough to forgive me for being such a snob.

My dad did all right with his broken ankle. He had plenty of time to read *all* the books on that shelf he'd been trying to reach and do his project for work. And my mother felt so sorry for him that she stopped complaining about his working. The O'Connells let us borrow the pickup truck whenever they weren't using it. That way my mother could drive my dad to the cove they liked so much, or over to the fisherman's dock. They seemed to be having a good enough vacation despite the cast and crutches.

I didn't see much of my parents, though. I spent most of my time with Mara. I was glad I'd brought so much candy. Mara and I shared it all. She especially liked apricot rolls, which she'd never had before. For the ten days that we were palling around together we each had one apricot roll a day.

I asked her to teach me a lot of the stuff she knew how to do, like how to steer that motorboat. On calm days my parents let me go out with her to check the lobster traps. It's a much easier job if there are two people.

I also told her I wanted to camp out.

"Let's wait for the full moon," she said. "That's tomorrow."

The next day we planned our sleepover. We wrote a menu for what we'd eat and a list of the supplies we'd need. We were going to cook all our meals over an open fire.

The night of the sleepover was one of the most memorable nights of my life. We had baked potatoes, hot dogs, and roasted corn on

Mara O'Connell and me. A friend for
two weeks that I'll never forget.

the cob. And since we'd saved the two plain chocolate bars I'd brought we were able to make s'mores. Then we laid out our sleeping bags on the very top of Blueberry Hill and slipped inside them. Above us was the full moon. It was so bright it was like daylight, only better because the light had a blue, moody quality. We could hear the surf crashing on the shore, and the smell of the pines was carried to us on soft, moist breezes. It made for an atmosphere that a person never forgets.

Mara and I talked for hours. I never knew the time because we didn't bring watches with us. We didn't need them because Mara knew the time by the position of the moon. (She also knew what time it was during the day just by checking out where the sun was.)

While we were lying there Mara told me spooky stories she'd heard about Pirate's Cove, and about the time her father was lost at sea for two whole days and nights.

I said, "Mara, you know so much and tell such great stories. I don't have anything to share with you."

She said, "Oh, Stacey, yes you do. Please, please tell me about Ireland. That's where my grandparents live and I've never met them. Tell me everything. And don't leave anything out."

I was glad I had something to share with

Mara. After that she asked me a lot of questions about living in New York City.

Two days later it was time to say good-bye to Pine Island and to Mara. Her mother was going to drive us and our stuff in the pickup over to the fisherman's dock. (Mara didn't drive us because she's only allowed to drive the pickup in an emergency. She thought that was a silly rule. At the time I did, too.) But we did use the two-way radio to tell Mr. Stanley to pick us up at the cove instead of at our dock.

I hated saying good-bye to Mara and to the island. We exchanged addresses. "Promise to write," I said.

"Every week," she replied. "Let's both say we'll write on Sunday afternoons."

"Yes," I said. "At three o'clock. That way we'll know the other person's doing it at the same time."

Mara nodded.

" 'Bye, Mara," I called as the boat pulled away from the dock and I left Pine Island forever.

" 'Bye, Stacey," she called back. By then the motor was roaring and we were headed out to sea, so I could barely hear her.

I never wrote a letter to Mara and she never wrote one to me. I started to write her, but I never finished. I'm sorry now that I didn't.

But I still remember that vacation as one of the most wonderful times of my life. It also taught me not to expect all people to be the same. I think it's because of that experience that I was able to adjust so well when we moved from New York City to Stoneybrook.

Pine Island and Mara taught me that new places and people can be an invitation to adventure.

WHEN I WAS TWELVE

CHAPTER 12

I was living in New York City again. It was a time in my life when I wished I could be in two places at once — in New York City with my parents and city friends, and in Stoneybrook with my Baby-sitters Club friends. I missed my Stoneybrook friends so much, especially Claudia Kishi.

One dreary Monday afternoon I was in my bedroom doing my homework . . .

I looked at the clock. Five-fifteen in the afternoon. In Stoneybrook my friends would be rushing to get to Claudia's in time for the Baby-sitters Club meeting. I missed being with them. I guess you could say I was feeling sorry for myself. So much so, in fact, that when the phone rang I was hoping it was Allison (whom I don't even like) inviting me to her birthday party.

"Stacey, Stacey! You'll never guess what!"

It was Claudia. Even though she sounded happy-excited and not upset-excited I said, "Claudia, is everything okay?"

"Everything's great!"

"So what's up? What won't I guess?" I was already feeling a hundred percent better than I had just a minute before.

"You'll never believe it," Claudia rushed on. "My parents said I can visit you in New York. I can take the train alone and everything. I had to beg like crazy but they said yes."

"Claudia, that's great!"

She was giggling. "I'm so excited that I forgot I haven't even been invited."

"Of course you're invited. You're always invited. When can you come? Can you come this weekend?"

"Don't you have plans and stuff? With Laine or something?"

136

"I don't have anything special planned. If I do anything with Laine, you can do it, too."

I was remembering a disastrous sleepover party when Claudia, Kristy, Mary Anne, and Dawn had come to New York City for the weekend. I thought it was a great chance for my Stoneybrook friends to meet my best New York friend. Claudia and Laine most definitely did not get along that night. Nobody got along. So you can imagine my surprise the next day when Laine (whose father, as I've mentioned, is a big deal Broadway producer) invited me and my Stoneybrook friends to go to a hit Broadway play. That night Laine and Claudia got along so well that when we were all saying thank-yous and good-byes, my two best friends exchanged addresses and phone numbers.

Now that Claudia was coming to New York maybe she and Laine would get to know one another even better and I wouldn't feel so split between my New York life and my old friends in Stoneybrook. I couldn't wait for Claudia to come.

"Claud, if you can possibly come this weekend, please, please do it."

"That's what I was hoping you'd say," she said, "because I can't wait to see you. Just a sec." I heard her say hi to Jessi and Mal as they arrived for the BSC meeting. I stayed on the phone long enough to say hello to everyone, but kept one eye on my watch. I knew that at five-thirty I had to be off the phone so clients could get through to the Baby-sitters Club. Claudia promised to call back as soon as the meeting was over.

I was so excited about Claudia's visit that I couldn't concentrate on my homework. I felt happier than I had been since we moved back to New York City.

To tell you the truth, things hadn't been so great at home. My parents thought they were hiding their problems from me, but I knew they weren't getting along. I was noticing more tension than ever between them. They were still together in those days, but it was hard to believe they were the same couple who spontaneously danced around the living room when I was eight and planned a vacation on a secluded island when I was ten. I noticed that they had stopped exchanging a hello kiss when my dad got home from work.

At school things weren't much better. Laine was still my best friend in New York. But my other good friends from Parker — Deirdre, Val, Sally, and Allison — weren't real friends anymore. My problems with them started even before I moved to Stoneybrook. In fact, one of the reasons I didn't mind moving to Stoneybrook in the first place was because

Parker Academy
grade 8
As self-confident
and sophisticated
as she looks.

Laine Cummings

Parker Academy
grade 8
Not as happy
as she looks.

Stacey McGill.

those girls were mean to me when I first learned I had diabetes. (I know it's hard to believe, but they were.)

Since I was back at Parker I felt like an outsider with them. For example, Allison was having a dinner party at a restaurant to celebrate her birthday and I wasn't invited. I was really glad Claudia was coming for the weekend.

The next day in the lunch line at school I told Laine about Claudia's visit. "Did you guys ever write to each other?" I asked.

"Were we supposed to?" Laine reached for her daily low-fat yogurt. That week she was determined to lose three pounds before she wore this black lycra mini-dress she'd bought for Allison's dinner party on Saturday night. "We're going to the Tribeca Bar and Grill," she told me. "You know, the actor Robert DeNiro's place in Tribeca." Then she leaned over and whispered, "Deirdre said she has a sore throat. Maybe she'll get sick and you can come in her place." Laine had already explained to me that the reason I wasn't invited was because Allison could only invite four guests. Of course, Laine, Val, Deirdre, and Sally came before me.

"It's no big deal," I said. "Besides, Claudia's coming. Maybe the three of us can go out Friday night. Or on Sunday. Or both. Let's plan something terrific for Claud. She's such fun."

Laine ignored my idea by saying, "I'm going back for a diet soda. Do you want one?"

We never did make plans together for Claudia's weekend in New York. Any time I brought up the subject Laine changed it. After school on Friday I told her I was hurrying home to get ready for Claudia. She said, "Have fun. See you on Monday!"

I didn't really care. Claudia was my best friend and I had a spectacular New York weekend planned for the two of us. Why shouldn't we have the most marvelous time? I thought.

But before Claudia arrived, I had an important errand. I may not be able to eat sugar, but Claudia can't live without it. So I bought her a weekend stash. I got chocolate bars with peanut butter filling, lollipops, M&M's, Gummi Bears, three kinds of chips, caramel popcorn, and Mallomars.

An hour later my mother and I took a cab to Grand Central to meet Claud. My mother was almost as excited as I was. She likes Claudia a lot and she knew that I wasn't enjoying my New York friends as much as my Stoneybrook friends. Mom and I had been waiting at the information booth in the big rotunda for about fifteen minutes when I squealed, "There she is."

Even in the rush hour crowd at Grand Central you couldn't miss Claud. She was the Japanese-American girl who looked as hip as any funky, downtown New Yorker. That day she had on a purple jacket, black tights, and red cowboy boots. Her black hair was half piled on her head and half down her back, so the brightly colored three-hoop earrings she'd made for herself showed off nicely. She was dragging a big suitcase on wheels. Knowing Claud she'd packed enough outfits to last a month. I ran to meet her.

By the time my mother reached us Claud and I were jumping up and down and hugging one another. (I kept an eye on her suitcase all the time. In a big city you can't be too careful.)

I talked a mile a minute in the cab, telling Claud what I'd planned for the weekend. While we were waiting at the curb in front of my building for the cabbie to take her big suitcase out of the trunk I said, "Of course we can do anything you want. New York's a big place and there's lots to do."

"You're the one who knows her way around," she said. "I'm the hick."

Before I could remind her how sophisticated she is, the cabbie put the suitcase on the sidewalk in front of us and said, "Staying for a while, eh?" We laughed about that as we bumped and rolled Claud's big suitcase into my apartment building. I was wishing that Claud could stay for a long time and imagined how much fun we'd have if she lived with me in New York City.

When we got to my room I told her to look under the pillow. "Mallomars!" she shrieked. Playing Hot and Cold, Claud hunted until she found the whole stash of junk food. Then she put everything back where I'd originally put it so she'd feel right at home. (She didn't hide the Mallomars because she was eating them.)

We both changed our clothes for dinner. My parents were taking us to the Saloon, a restaurant with roller-skating waiters (and a great menu). The Saloon is across from Lincoln Center so it's a perfect spot for people-watching. My mother came to my room to tell us that my father wouldn't be going to dinner with us. She sounded very annoyed. "He's such a workaholic," she said. "I shouldn't be surprised."

After my mother left, Claud said, "I was looking forward to seeing your father."

"You'll see him plenty because you're here *all* weekend, remember?" We just grinned at one another.

When we left for dinner my mother was in a bad mood because my dad had canceled on us. Fortunately she improved quickly. But as we window-shopped along Columbus Avenue I started to notice that now Claudia was in a bad mood. There are fifteen store-filled blocks between our apartment building and the Saloon restaurant. We were stopping and checking out every window. In the Betsey Johnson store window I pointed out the lycra dress that Laine had bought. Claudia didn't seem very impressed with it and moved on to the next store window. "Tomorrow let's go back to Betsey Johnson's," I said. "And you can try some stuff on. It's your kind of store."

"Not really," she replied.

I didn't say anything because just then we bumped into a bunch of kids from my school. I introduced Claud to Jason, Wilson, Emily, and Melissa, who told us they were on their way to a movie and then were going bowling.

When they left I thought Claud would say something like, "Bowling in New York City? Boy, you can do everything here." But she didn't. So I said it. I couldn't understand why she was being so negative and grumpy.

Claud seemed more like herself at dinner. Mom and I asked her about Stoneybrook and our friends there. And I was right about Claud loving the Saloon.

After dinner we strolled around Lincoln

Center. Then we walked back on the east side of Columbus Avenue so we could look in the stores we'd missed coming down. It wasn't fun, though, because Claud was a drag again. I'd say, "Look at that hat. It would be perfect on you." And she'd say, "Oh," or just grunt.

When we got back to the apartment we went to my room to hang out. Before I had a chance to ask Claudia what was wrong she turned into the old Claud and we had a great time. First I tried on some of those clothes she'd brought. Then we looked through magazines. But the most important thing we did was talk, talk, talk. And finally it felt like the good old days when Claudia and I were in Stoneybrook.

CHAPTER 13

The first thing I noticed when I woke the next morning was that someone was sleeping in my room and that that someone was Claudia. The second thing I noticed was that the sun was shining and the sky was the cloudless bright blue that promises a long, beautiful day. Claud likes to sleep late, but it was already nine-thirty and I had planned a full day for us. I stared at her and whispered, "Claud, wake up," until she opened her eyes. And closed them again.

I heard someone come in the front door and remembered my mother saying she'd get us fresh bagels. I jumped out of bed and ran into the hall. Before she got to the kitchen I took a hot sesame bagel out of the bag and returned to my room to wave that bagel in front of Claud's nose. She got up. My dad had just gotten up, too, so we all had our bagel breakfast together. "They don't get any better or fresher than this," I told Claudia. She didn't say, "You're right. They're fabulous," like I thought she would. But she did eat two.

After breakfast we took showers, picked out what we were going to wear, and got dressed. By the time we left the house it was eleven o'clock. "Almost time for lunch," Claudia joked. She was eating a chocolate bar when she said it.

Since it was a sunny day we walked through Central Park to the Metropolitan Museum of Art. I described how in New York there are free concerts in Central Park put on by the New York Philharmonic Orchestra and the New York City Opera. I told her how stars like Diana Ross and Paul Simon had performed not far from where we were standing. Claud wasn't impressed.

Then I pointed to a ballfield where some kids were playing touch football. "That's the field where my physical education class comes to play soccer," I explained. "A lot of schools use the park for their phys ed activities. Isn't that neat?"

All she said was, "Too bad you have to walk so far just for a phys ed class."

Uh-oh, I thought, whatever was eating Claud yesterday is back. But I knew that being in the Metropolitan Museum of Art would improve her mood. And it did.

I thought she'd want to go right to the well-known galleries, like twentieth-century painting. But Claudia's first stop was ancient jewelry. She stood in front of a glass case and stared at an ivory loop earring the size of an orange. There wasn't any post on it. I decided a hole big enough for that earring to go through would be the size of a dime. Meanwhile Claud was absorbed in how the earring was carved. She whispered in wonder, "Look how intricate it is."

"But think how big the hole in a person's ear would have to be," I said.

"It's not an earring."

"Oh, good," I said.

"It's a nose ring."

I gasped in disgust, but Claudia didn't think that was gross at all.

We looked at some more ancient jewelry before going to twentieth-century painting.

As we were leaving the Met I reminded her, "We're going to John's for pizza. It's the best pizza in New York. They cook it in a brick oven. Everybody goes there. Okay?"

"Sure," Claud said. "Why not?" She seemed incredibly bored by the idea.

When we got outside she took out her camera and clicked off a few pictures of the museum and of me on the steps. I may look happy in the pictures, but I wasn't. I was con-

Claudia's photo of me on the steps of
the Metropolitan Museum of Art.

fused. One second I was with the old Claud. The next second I was with a grumpy stranger. While we were waiting for the bus I asked her, "What's wrong, Claud?"

"What do you mean?"

"I just told you about this great place for pizza and you acted like it's not a big deal."

"Well, really, Stace, it isn't. We do have pizza in Stoneybrook you know."

That's when the bus came, so we hopped on. We took side-by-side seats. I told Claudia to sit by the window so she'd have a good view of the city as we rode downtown. As the bus moved along I told her the story of how Laine and I had skipped ballroom dance classes and taken this same bus route to FAO Schwarz. "And there's the Plaza Hotel," I continued, "where my parents took me for my fourth birthday."

She didn't seem interested, but I persisted. I pointed out Saks Fifth Avenue and St. Patrick's Cathedral. Even though Claud had seen some of these places before and I'd seen them dozens of times, it's neat to see them one after the other as you go downtown on the bus. Claudia didn't seem to be enjoying the trip at all.

She did seem to like the pizza, but she didn't have much energy for talking. I was beginning to wonder if she was getting sick. Finally I gave up trying to keep up a conversation and ate my pizza in silence, too. When we were back in the street I asked her if she wanted to go back to my place to rest before we went out for the night.

"Sure," she said. "Why not?"

"Why not?" I answered. The frustration I was feeling toward her came out in my voice. "Because maybe there are some other things you'd like to do. We *are* in New York City, you know."

"You keep making such a big deal about that," Claud said. "New York's not that far from Stoneybrook. I've been here before, you know, and I'll be here again."

"So we'll go home," I said. I went to the curb and raised my arm. "I'll hail a cab."

"We don't have to take a cab," Claudia said. "We can take a subway. Or don't you want me to see that some parts of New York aren't so 'neat' and 'great' and 'fantastic.' "

"Fine, fine, sure," I said. "If that's what you want to do. I'm not ashamed of the subway. I like the subway. It's great. Come on." I headed down the street without looking to see if Claud was following.

The train was crowded and we had to stand. We hardly spoke during the trip. I stopped being a tour guide, which was easy enough since we were underground and there wasn't much to see.

My mother was at a matinee movie with Mrs. Cummings, and my father was (you guessed it) at his office. I checked the answering machine for messages while Claudia threw herself across the couch to continue being glum. I wasn't even looking forward to the evening.

The first message was from Kristy. "Hey, guys, just called to say hello. Hope you're having a great time. That was silly to say. I *know* you're having a great time. The other reason I called was to remind Claudia that she's sitting for the Barretts after school on Monday. 'Bye, Stace. 'Bye, Claud. See ya.''

It was so good to hear Kristy's voice that Claudia and I exchanged a smile. But the next message killed it.

"Hi, Stacey. It's Allison. Listen, I know it's the last minute and everything but I'm having this dinner party tonight at the Tribeca Bar and Grill. Robert DeNiro's place. I'd love for you to come. Let me know, okay? Oh, yeah, and it's dressy — not formal but fancy. 'Bye.''

"Thanks a lot, Allison," I said to the machine. "What a joke."

Claudia was standing now. "You can go to the party, Stacey. I'll stay here. I'm sort of tired anyway."

"I didn't say it's a joke because you're here.

The joke is that Allison doesn't even like me and I don't particularly like her. She's just asking me because Deirdre got sick or something and she wants to fill out the table. Laine probably told her to invite me."

Claudia said, "You're not going because of me. You probably had to change all kinds of interesting plans."

"I didn't. Claud, will you stop that? I invited you here, didn't I?"

"I invited myself."

The rest of the evening didn't go much better. We went to a six-thirty movie. It was a comedy, but I didn't hear much laughter from Claudia. I wasn't laughing either. I was thinking I'd be having a better time at Allison's party. It would certainly be more interesting than being with Claudia. Besides, since I was living in New York weren't those the friendships I should be cultivating?

During the last part of the movie I started to feel like my blood sugar was out of whack. I needed to eat. As soon as the movie was over I told Claudia I was a little late on my eating schedule and I was beginning to feel it. (When you have diabetes you have to eat regularly. It had been a while since we'd had lunch.)

Claudia became very concerned for me and pushed us through the crowd leaving the theater (like a true New Yorker). There's a good Chinese restaurant across the street from the movie theater so we went over there. As the waitress showed us to a table Claudia said, "Could we have an order of sesame noodles right away, please, and then we'll order the rest."

"Thanks," I told Claud. None of the girls eating at the Tribeca Bar and Grill that night would have been that thoughtful. Not even Laine. My diabetes gave them the creeps.

As soon as I ate I started to feel better, but I could see that something was bothering Claud again.

"What's been bugging you, Claud?" I asked. "Don't you like New York?"

"It's okay," she said. "Maybe I'm coming down with a cold or something." But she didn't sneeze or cough or have runny eyes. She just looked and acted depressed, and as if she didn't particularly want to be with me.

We dragged ourselves home. Claudia rallied a little to report to my parents on our day. But when we got to my room she said she wanted to go right to bed.

I couldn't believe this was happening. My best friend whom I hardly ever got to be with was here and we were having a terrible time. I was going to ask her if there was something special she wanted to do the next day, but it didn't seem to be the right topic. Maybe she just wanted to go home.

I turned off the lights and got into bed. I lay there thinking about all that had happened since Claudia had gotten off the train. I couldn't for the life of me figure out what I'd done wrong. Wasn't I the same friend I'd been to her in Stoneybrook? Tears came into my eyes. I'd been so happy and excited about this weekend and it had turned out to be so rotten. I didn't mind not having fun and I certainly didn't care that I'd missed Allison's party. What I really minded was losing my best friend. That's when I thought I understood what was wrong. Claudia didn't like me anymore. I had to know if it was true.

"Come, on, Claud," I whispered. "Tell me what's wrong. Just tell me the truth. I can take it."

Claudia burst into tears.

CHAPTER 14

I sat next to Claudia. "Tell me what's wrong. Please."

She sniffled and cried but didn't say anything. I handed her a Kleenex, "You've got to or I'll go 'crazy mad out of my mind.' "

She couldn't help but smile at that because "You've got to or I'll go crazy mad out of my mind," is something Marilyn Arnold says when she wants one of her baby-sitters to do something for her.

"Claudia," I said, "if you don't want to be my friend anymore, just come out and say it."

With that Claudia bolted upright in bed. "Not be your friend? That's the last thing I want. Don't you understand, Stace? You're the first best friend I've ever had. You've had Laine since you were little kids. And you still have each other." She stopped to blow her nose. I tried to say something, but she held up her hand to tell me not to speak. "Before you," she continued, "I never had a best friend. And now I've lost you and I'm wrecked. I'm the one who's going 'crazy mad out of my mind.' "

"Oh, Claudia," I said. "But you are my best friend. You haven't lost me. Is that why you've been acting so weird? How could you think I wasn't still your friend. What'd I do?"

"You didn't do anything. It's just that I hate that you live in this dumb old city. Every place we go, especially places I know you love, I think, 'this is where Stacey lives. These are her friends. These are the places she visits. She doesn't live in Stoneybrook anymore and she never will.' I miss you so much," she continued. "This weekend is just reminding me of how much. While you're having a wonderful time here I'm miserable in Stoneybrook. How could you leave me?"

That's when I told Claudia how much I missed her. And all the things that were going wrong in my life since I came back to New York. How my parents weren't getting along and how I didn't like the kids that used to be my friends at Parker. "I'm miserable, too, Claud," I said. "That's why I was looking forward to this weekend so much."

"I'm sorry I've ruined it for you," she said. "I am, Stace. But I feel better because I told you what's been on my mind."

"I feel better, too," I said. "And the good news is that the weekend isn't over yet. We have tomorrow."

We lay in bed talking about what we could do the next day. The last thing I heard before I fell asleep was, "And maybe we could go to that Betsey Johnson store. You're right, it's my kind of place."

The next morning I opened my eyes to see Claudia sitting cross-legged on the end of my bed sucking on a lollipop. "Up and at 'em," she said. "Let's not waste a minute."

I looked at the clock. Eight o'clock on Sunday morning. I told her, "Nothing's open but diners."

"So let's go to one. I love diners. The funkier the better." Claud pulled my sheet off. "Come on, sleepyhead. During breakfast we'll make a list of everything we're going to do today so we don't forget anything. But we better get going."

We walked up and down Broadway until Claudia was satisfied that we were going to the most genuine diner. While she ate a heap of pancakes and sausages I had eggs and toast. Then we wrote out the list.

At the top of the list was the Central Park Zoo. We were the first in line when it opened. As we visited the exhibits Claud kept saying how much the kids she sits for in Stoneybrook would like certain animals. That made me a little sad because I missed those kids so much, especially Charlotte Johanssen who adores polar bears. And I knew that Matt Braddock would be fascinated with the penguins. When we came out of the penguin house Claudia spotted an artist making pastel portraits of people for ten dollars.

"I want to have her do your portrait," she said. "Do you mind sitting for it? It'll be my souvenir."

"Only if you'll sit for one, too," I said.

We watched while the artist finished up the portrait she was doing of a little boy. Then it was my turn. I had a brilliant idea. I asked the artist, "Would you do us together?"

"A double portrait," she said. "Of best friends, I bet."

Claudia and I exchanged a smile. "Very best friends," I said.

While the artist was drawing us, Claudia asked her about her training. That was interesting. Being drawn in public was a little embarrassing, though, because people would stop to watch us. But all in all it was a nice experience, especially because I knew that Claudia would have that picture to remind her what great friends we are, even if we didn't live in the same city.

"What's next?" I asked Claudia.

Claudia Kishi and Stacey McGill.
Friends forever.

She checked the list. "The Museum of Modern Art. Do you mind?"

"Are you kidding? I love that museum." I stopped myself before I said, "I go there all the time," because I didn't want to remind Claudia that I ♥ New York.

At the museum we saw a fascinating exhibit of collages. I could tell that Claudia was very inspired by it. She even got some ideas for things to add to her Kid-Kit. (A Kid-Kit is a box of art supplies, books, and games that each BSC member brings to baby-sitting jobs.) "And," Claudia continued, "I'm going to design a line of personal stationery with little collages in the left-hand corner."

Next on our list was lunch at the Hard Rock Cafe. On the way there we passed a five and dime store. "Let's check it out," Claudia said. "These places have great junk jewelry that I can take apart and use in my own pieces." In a bin marked "79¢ each/priced to sell" Claudia found four things that she could use.

Before we took them to the cash register I spotted a photo booth. We grinned at one another and said, "Let's." We took two strips of photos so we'd each have one.

For once there wasn't a line at the Hard Rock Cafe so we walked right in. I love to look at all the rock and roll memorabilia on the walls and of course listen to the great music. But that music didn't keep Claudia and me from talking every minute we had left together. Fun talk and serious talk. It really made me feel better to let someone know what was going on between my parents, and to tell Claudia again about what an outsider I was at school. And Claudia got a chance to bring me up to date on her problems with schoolwork and her feelings of inferiority when she's around her sister, who's a genuine genius. I can't remember exactly what the fun talk was about, just that I had that happy, secure feeling you get when you've had a chance to talk and laugh with your best friend.

When we came out of the restaurant it was time to head back to the apartment for Claud's suitcase. Her train was leaving at five. But we still had enough time to stop at the Betsey Johnson store. Claudia tried on a couple of things and bought a pair of black-and-lime-green-striped leggings on sale for eight dollars.

When Claudia got on the train at Grand Central Station she had a bunch of souvenirs to take back to Stoneybrook that would remind her of our friendship: the photo strip, a pastel drawing of the two of us, some junk jewelry, and a pair of wild leggings that she'd never have found in Stoneybrook.

Me? I had my memory of our talks that weekend and of what an extra special best friend I had in Claudia. Those were the souvenirs I took home with me that afternoon. Oh, yes, and my favorite photos ever of Claudia and me.

The period after Claudia's visit was very difficult and confusing for me. More than once I wished with all my heart that Claudia lived nearby so I could see her whenever I wanted. My parents were having more and more problems. They even saw a marriage counselor. And do you know what the marriage counselor told them? That they should probably get divorced, which is what they decided to do.

The decision I got to make was which parent I wanted to live with. Since that was an impossible decision to make, I turned it into a decision about where I wanted to live. Once I looked at it that way I realized that as much as I ♥ New York I wanted to live in the same town as my very best friend and to be back in the Baby-sitters Club.

So here I am in Stoneybrook writing my autobiography.

THE END

CHAPTER 15

I've been rereading my autobiography and adding photos and memorabilia to it for a couple of hours now. I think it's almost done.

I learned a lot about myself from writing down these experiences as well as from remembering a lot of other experiences that aren't in my autobiography.

As I read it over I am amazed at how similar my thirteen-year-old self is to my younger self. It's impossible for me to imagine that I could have acted any differently than I did. I can see why I wasn't being particularly nice to Mara on Pine Island when I was ten. I can understand how much I upset my parents by not going to those ballroom dancing classes when I was eight. I remember how disappointed I was that I wasn't on television in the Thanksgiving Day parade when I was five. I can even understand why I didn't figure out why Claudia was so upset when she came to visit me in New York.

I understand why I acted the way I did when these things happened. It was just me, Stacey McGill, being Stacey McGill.

The thing that I see the most in my auto-biography is that I am a very lucky person to have such great parents, great places to live, and wonderful friends.

Now that I've pretty much finished this as-signment I'm getting nervous that my teacher won't like it. I always feel this way when I hand in a big assignment, so I'll probably have the jitters about it all weekend.

I wonder how Claudia's autobiography is coming along. I hope she'll let me read it. It'll be fun to see if she's writing as much about me as I wrote about her. Reading about Clau-dia in my autobiography makes me want to see her. If I leave right now for the Baby-sitters Club meeting I can get to Claudia's ten min-utes early. That'll give us some time to gab before the others arrive.

I sure hope nothing too interesting happens to me on the way to Claudia's. I don't want to have to add anything to my autobiog-raphy!

ASSIGNMENT: Autobiography
STUDENT: Stacey McGill
TEACHER COMMENTS:

I enjoyed reading your autobiography. You worked hard on this assignment and it shows. You have used good organization, keen descriptions, and good analysis of what your experiences meant to you.

GRADE: *A*

About the Author

ANN M. MARTIN did *a lot* of baby-sitting when she was growing up in Princeton, New Jersey. She is a former editor of books for children, and was graduated from Smith College.

Ms. Martin lives in New York City with her cats, Mouse and Rosie. She likes ice cream and *I Love Lucy*; and she hates to cook.

Ann Martin's Apple Paperbacks include *Yours Turly, Shirley*; *Ten Kids, No Pets*; *With You and Without You*; *Bummer Summer*; and all the other books in the Baby-sitters Club series.

**Read all the books
about Stacey
in the Baby-sitters Club series
by Ann M. Martin**

THE BABY-SITTERS CLUB®

by Ann M. Martin

More titles... ▶

The Baby-sitters Club titles continued...

Available wherever you buy books...or use this order form.

Scholastic Inc., P.O. Box 7502, 2931 E. McCarty Street, Jefferson City, MO 65102

Please send me the books I have checked above. I am enclosing $_____
(please add $2.00 to cover shipping and handling). Send check or money order - no
cash or C.O.D.s please.

Name _____ Birthdate_____

Address _____

City_____ State/Zip_____
Please allow four to six weeks for delivery. Offer good in the U.S. only. Sorry, mail orders are not
available to residents of Canada. Prices subject to change.

Ann Martin wants *YOU* to help name the new baby-sitter...and her twin.

Dear Diary,
I'm 13 now...finally in the 8th grade. My twin sister and I just moved here and this great group of girls asked me to join their baby-sitting club...

Name the twins and win a

THE BABY-SITTERS CLUB

book dedication!

Simply dream up the first and last names of the new baby-sitter and her twin sister (who's not in the BSC), and fill in the names on the coupon below. One lucky entry will be selected by Ann M. Martin and Scholastic Inc. The winning names will continue to be featured in the series starting next fall 1995, and the winner will have a future BSC book dedicated to her/him!

Just fill in the coupon below or write the information on a 3"x 5" piece of paper and mail to: THE BSC NAME THE TWINS CONTEST: Scholastic Inc., P.O. Box 7500, 2931 E. McCarty Street, Jefferson City, MO 65102. Entries must be postmarked by January 31, 1995. No purchase necessary. Enter as often as you wish, one entry to an envelope. Mechanically reproduced entries are void. Scholastic is not responsible for late, lost or postage due mail. Contest open to residents of the U.S.A. 6-15 years upon entering. Employees of Scholastic Inc., it's agencies, affiliates, subsidiaries and their families are ineligible. Winners will be selected at random from all official entries received and notified by mail. Winners will be required to execute an eligibility affidavit to release the use of their names for any promotional purposes determined by Scholastic Inc. Winners are responsible for all taxes that may be attached to any prize winnings. Prizes may be substituted by Scholastic Inc. For a complete list of winners, send a self-addressed, stamped envelope after January 31, 1995 to: The BSC NAME THE TWINS CONTEST Winners List at the address provided above.

THE BSC NAME THE TWINS CONTEST

Name the new twins! (First and last, please)

_____ **and** _____

Name _____   Birthdate _____
                                              M / D / Y
Street _____ City _____ State/Zip _____

BSCC1194